HIGHWAY OF FEAR

HIGHWAY OF FEAR

Helen McCabe

First published in the UK by Chivers Press, 2012

This edition published in 2015 by
Telos Moonrise: Romantic Encounters
(An imprint of Telos Publishing Ltd)
5A Church Road, Shortlands, Bromley, Kent BR2 0HP

www.telos.co.uk

Telos Publishing Ltd values feedback. Please e-mail us with any comments you may have about this book to:
feedback@telos.co.uk

1

'You're kidding. Here, let me look!' Gina grabbed the letter out of her father's hand and began to scan the neat, upright strokes that proclaimed Mark Baxter's handwriting. She couldn't believe that her ex-boyfriend and boss had had the nerve to write to her father suggesting he should stop her going on the trip she'd been planning for so long. 'This is absolutely ludicrous! Does he think it's the 19th Century?'

The cheek of the man! He was positively medieval. She'd found out that Mark was a control freak a long time ago, but this capped everything. She glared across at her father and threw down the letter on the coffee table.

'Well,' Colin said, his mouth twitching, as if he was going to burst out laughing, 'he's deadly serious. I don't like the man, but you've really upset him, Gina. Did you have to ditch the Chairman's son just before I got my promotion?'

She was used to his teasing, but this hit a nerve. 'Don't worry, Dad,' blazed Gina, who had a short fuse. 'I suppose you think I went out with Mark in the first place just because you didn't like him!' She knew that wasn't fair, but she felt so uptight she had to get up and walk over to the window. The letter was most certainly the final straw in their relationship, which had been rocky for some time.

Initially they'd been thrown together through work. Gina realised now that she'd gone out with him because it had seemed the right thing to do at the time. Now she knew better. How could she have been such a fool? Mark and she had different agendas. He was a staid 35 who was set in his ways, while Gina, at 23, felt life was definitely for living – and the more it was filled with excitement, the better.

She sighed then, thinking about the effect of his stupid letter on her father. Colin had never stood in her way over anything. And now, today, when she'd been psyching herself up to broach the subject dearest to her heart – her trip into the Xingu rainforest – Mark had dropped this bombshell. Damn him! She clenched her fists.

'Come on, explain to me then?' her father persisted from across the room.

'He's gone mad,' she snapped.

When she swung round, her father's merry expression had turned to hurt. Suddenly Gina felt an extraordinary rush of sympathy for her dad, who was reaching for a cigarette. He lit up and inhaled deeply. Usually, Gina would have told him off for breaking the resolution to quit he made every New Year. But this wasn't the time. She breathed in, ready to fight her corner, as he put his feet up on the coffee table and puffed, staring up at the ceiling.

She knew instinctively that on the surface Colin was trying to appear relaxed, while deep down he was living the kind of hell any father dreads; the moment when his only daughter is about to tell him she's going to walk out and do exactly what she wants in life – however much he's against it. An awkward silence ensued.

A moment later, he asked, 'Do you want talk about it?' He drew in the smoke to calm his nerves. He'd tried to give up many times, but this wasn't one of them.

'Not really,' she said. 'In fact, there's nothing to tell. Mark and I are finished. I suppose he thought this was a way of getting himself noticed again. He won't take no for an answer.'

'He says here that you're about to go off to the Xingu. Are you?' She didn't answer. 'I can see why he's scared. I am too.'

Colin was trying to get to the truth and be tactful at the same time, which was hardly his style. He'd spent most of his time with men who wouldn't recognise the meaning of tact, especially in connection with their families. Big businessmen like him who, in a lot of cases, were rarely at home; and who, when anything went wrong personally, didn't understand why, or didn't care. But he was different.

'I *am* going, Dad!' she said.

Colin exhaled, letting the news sink in. He was deeply worried now. All he had to hang on to was that Gina might see common sense. At least, she'd ditched Mark Baxter, who would never have been his choice for her! On the other hand, he had a horrible feeling that now, he would never dissuade her from going. Mark's letter had seen to that. She was like Colin himself. If someone told him forcefully enough not to do something, he usually took no notice.

'I'm sorry, Dad,' she said, looking straight at him.

Gina had lovely dark-blue eyes, fringed with the blackest of lashes. She was so like Carol that it made him gasp. But her mother had been dark. Gina had got her blonde hair from him. He passed a hand over his close-cropped head. His own blond days were over.

But those eyes of Gina's were warm now and, at that moment, full of sympathy for her old dad. She'd always been like quicksilver; able to handle so many things at once. She reminded him of a beautiful rainbow, so brightly coloured when it appeared, and when it faded he was never sure it would come back. But all the colours were there now. And, so far, they had kept on returning to warm up his life.

Colin had suspected that when a bloke fell in love with his Gina, he was bound to fall hard. For one minute, he almost pitied Baxter. Then he squashed the feeling. The man could be a real swine.

'I'll be okay, you know,' she said, sitting down and sprawling in her favourite chair opposite him. 'I'm a big girl now.' She pushed a heavy swathe of blonde hair back from her forehead. Now those blue eyes had a devilish glint in them.

Ever since she and her father had settled in Brazil and she'd discovered the existence of the Xingu forest, she'd wanted to go trekking there. She and her friends had talked about it incessantly; but, in the end, they all knew it was only Gina who had the nerve to try it.

Besides, she wanted exclusive photographs of a place no-one had ever been to before. If it contained photos of the Xingu, the book she'd been writing for the last year, about her life in Brazil, would be a cert for publication.

She smiled. 'Don't worry about Mark and me. It's over. I never liked him enough to be serious; and how he had the nerve to write to you, I've no idea. He's ...' She didn't how to describe him, except as a control freak. 'He's obsessive.'

'He writes like he owns you.' Colin flipped the letter over, his relief betraying itself in the careless gesture. Gina knew her father had been scared that she and Mark would fall in love.

'Well, he doesn't own me, and he never will.'

'I suppose I'll have to answer the damn thing!' Colin scratched his head.

'I suppose you will.' Suddenly she giggled. Colin looked at her sharply. 'Sorry! But it is funny. I was fuming at first, but now ... How dare he?'

'The poor sod was in love with you, I expect,' muttered Colin.

'Now don't go feeling sorry for him, Dad. You know what he's really like.'

She placed a butterfly kiss on his cheek. At least he had tact and sense enough not to invade her privacy by asking just exactly what had happened between the two of them. They might have been to bed together, but Mark certainly hadn't been the love of her life. He was good-looking, with striking features, but he was also arrogant.

On the other hand, he was extremely wealthy, and from the outside, they'd looked the perfect couple. But there was a coldness about him that occasionally frightened her. If she hadn't been the kind of girl she was, Mark could quite easily have taken control of her life. No, Gina had learned her lesson the hard way, and was off men at the moment.

But, deep down, she knew that it wouldn't stay like that. She needed to be loved. To feel the excitement of love and making love again. But with the right man this time.

From now on, she would be looking for more than entangling herself with someone for the sake of it. Secretly, she thought that most of the men she'd seen since she had come to Belem were there for the lap-dancing. Yet she knew she still hoped that one day she'd find a man to be at the centre of her world; a man to fulfil all her dreams. But she hadn't met him yet. And Mark was definitely not *the one*. How could she have ever thought he was?

'Well, I'd better get on.' Colin pressed the top of his ball-point and signed the report he'd been reading before he'd opened the offending post marked 'Personal'. He placed the letter inside his briefcase and smiled at his daughter. 'I'm glad you and Mark are finished. I've never thought that he was right for you.'

'Well, thank you for not saying so,' she replied.

He stood up, walked to his desk and leafed through the rest of the morning's post. At least she'd said that she didn't want him. The good relationship he felt he shared with his daughter was something he prized. He hadn't wanted to spoil it by prying.

'Let's forget the whole thing, shall we?' Gina smiled.

'We'll do that,' said Colin, 'just as soon as I've answered him. In my own way.' He lit another cigarette, exhaled air, then grinned back. Thank God that was over. He thought again how like her mother she was.

'I'd like you to approve of my trek, Dad?'

'Why should I? You know it's too dangerous.'

'I'll be careful. You can find a good guide for me.'

'Can I?' He tried to hide his anxiety with a mixture of amusement and nonchalance.

'Don't play games with me, Dad, it doesn't suit you. I've made up my mind. If I'm ever to write about the Xingu, I have to spend some time in there – before you and the company ruin what's left of Brazil!'

'You've already seen it from the air!'

Gina raised sceptical eyebrows. 'Now you're not playing

fair! You know I want to see it from *ground level* and not from a plane.'

'That's even more dangerous.' Colin tried to be calm.

Her expression changed to a bolder, defiant one as she tried another tack. 'At least it'll get me away from Mark.'

'I even prefer Baxter to the forest.' The idea of her disappearing into the Xingu terrified him.

Gina was silent for a moment, then added wryly, 'You don't mean that, Dad.'

'Maybe I do!' he teased back. 'After all, like father, like daughter! And who cares if we've just blown a good business merger – the Chairman's son and the Chief Surveyor's daughter?'

Gina slipped her arm through his, cajoling him now just as successfully as she had done when she was *his* little girl. He liked the feel of her next to him. No woman could take her place. After Carol had died, he had taken a job in Brazil. It was an exciting country. There was nothing in Belem – that ocean city, the gateway to the Amazon – that in any way resembled home.

At first it had been perfect. The great central valley of the Amazon basin hadn't then started its run from man's encroachment. In the early days, few people had considered the implications of cutting down the world's forests. Things were changing – and fast! The whole rainforest debate that had suddenly seemed to be on everyone's lips was now easing off again. But not for the people who were affected.

'The plane could easily drop me at Cachimbo. And Martin Wessler is sure to know of a good guide.'

'I suppose I could sound him out!'

'Thanks, Dad!' She brushed his cheek with a grateful little kiss.

'I could come too.'

'You know you'd hate it!' She put her arms around him. 'It isn't that I don't want you along ...'

He laughed. 'I know damn well you don't want me along! And who can blame you? Go on your crazy adventure, girl, but come back in one piece!'

'I will! Now, how about some coffee?' His Portuguese secretary didn't come in very early.

'That must be the most sensible idea you've come up with all morning!'

Gina grinned.

It wasn't until he'd had lunch with his colleague Martin Wessler, who'd enlightened him about the best guide to accompany Gina, that Colin made his choice. After hearing the German's opinion of maverick Rafe Perez, an aristocratic half-English/Portuguese, he had already decided to insist on another woman going along on the trip. As he'd said to Martin, 'I don't want my Gina wandering off into God knows where with a parcel of men. What's Perez like with women?'

'I think you're very wise,' Martin replied, 'but Perez is a loner. They say he's not interested in Europeans, and he certainly wouldn't compromise his position with the company by any fooling around. He also recently lost his partner, a native girl, Dorita, in a river accident on an expedition to the Aucas, and he seems not to have got over it. But he's the best!'

'You'll have to tell me that story sometime,' replied Colin.

'Yes, I think you might be very interested, as it concerns Mark Baxter!'

'Baxter?'

'I hear that he was too spineless to risk getting near the girl's raft, while Perez had already been swept away downriver. He could have helped her but he lost his nerve, froze like a rabbit, and the girl drowned.'

'Poor kid,' replied Colin.

2

On the downtown side of Belem city, close to the river, the Paradiso Bar was the place for business meetings of the shady sort. A place to play blackjack or roulette and discuss all kinds of traffic. It was a popular place for locals, the haunt of sailors and a special kind of tourists, who had been brought there by their guides for a little local colour and the quality of the lap-dancing.

Perez had never frequented the Paradiso. He liked cleaner places. But he had arranged to meet two people there that he couldn't do without if he was going to take on the latest trek for Baxter-Weber Incorporated ... So he was sitting at the bar at 10.00 as arranged.

No woman, married or single, who passed through the Paradiso that night was able to resist a furtive glance at the handsome, dark-haired guy. Perez was that kind of man. Women couldn't help looking at the tall, hard-muscled frame and imagining what he'd be like in bed. But if you caught his glance, a *frisson* of electricity would spark through you, rising from the depth of the darkest of Latin eyes. And, near to, Perez resembled a lithe wild animal, dangerous but beautiful.

That evening, Perez was tense and watchful, his face gave nothing away, and when he moved, it was quickly and silently, with a controlled power that made men move out of his way – and women pause to look again.

A bar girl was staring at him now; a beauty with a creamy skin and a body that most men would die for. She was clearly attracted, as her eyes swept over him, taking in his broad chest and long muscular legs in their cotton slacks. What she found most entrancing of all was his *insouciant* air, as if he had no idea of his effect on the female sex.

Her dark eyes flickered, offering him an open invitation; but, although conscious of her gaze, Perez merely lifted his head and glanced away – as if she didn't exist. He signalled indifferently for a waiter to bring him a drink. The girl didn't interest him. Since Dorita, girls meant nothing. Perez cared only about the forest now. It was only in the wonderful green darkness that he felt he was alive.

That night, Perez's riveting eyes were gloomy as he waited for Sinon. He would rather have done the trek without him, but the Greek was useful – he had influence with the Indian chief, Santana. And when Perez took off from the highway to the settlement in the forests, he wanted nothing to go wrong this time.

Perez despised Sinon for his lack of scruples. He knew how few the man had, when it came to deadly trafficking in big game. It was all the same to Sinon, alive or dead. Legal protection had reduced the slaughter, but there were still poachers like the Greek around. Poachers who would think nothing of destroying animals like ocelots, jaguars and margays. They made huge profits from their work. The pelts sold easily on the black markets of the world, and the thought of it made Perez sick. But, whatever else the Greek dealt in, was probably wise to leave alone.

His frown deepened. How he hated all that was happening around him. Soon there would be nothing! No seas of waving trees nor bright parrot flashes! Nothing but waste and emptiness! And they called it progress! Deforestation, *progress?*

That's why he had jumped at the chance to go back into the Xingu. So far, the area had been left alone. He wondered about the girl he was taking along. Would she be able to stand it? The Xingu was wet and hot! So wet and hot that when you hung up your damp clothes at night, they were still the same in the morning.

A rare smile flickered about his mouth. The girl he was detailed to take had to be brave to take it on. And, what was more important, her father was paying a lot of money for his services.

Yes, he'd agree to the trek because he intended to make as much as he could out of just another company that was murdering the rainforest, however much it tried to hide the fact. Perez felt like the Indians did – that he was being pushed out of the only place he could call home.

He looked up. His old flame, Elena, was making her way toward him. Her hair was black, but her skin was fair. Her fingers were loaded with rings, and her expensive dress was made from raw silk and slashed almost to the thigh. That he had to take another woman along to keep the little rich girl happy was part of the company's deal, but he wished it could have been someone else. But Elena was used to the forests, and Sinon wouldn't come without her. The fact was, the Greek didn't trust her enough to leave her behind. Perez had turned to Elena himself once when he'd been lonely and grieving for Dorita. But he'd found no real comfort.

'Elena.'

'*Perez*! How lovely to see you after all this time.'

'Where's Sinon?' Perez ignored the girl's embrace.

'I haven't got the plague!' Elena laughed sarcastically.

'I've a lot on my mind,' he replied curtly.

'You used to be much warmer, darling.'

'That was a long time ago. Where's Sinon?' he repeated.

'Patience. He's over there. But I wish he wasn't.'

'Cut it out, Elena,' Perez ordered. 'I'm not interested; and, for both our sakes, you'd better watch what you're saying.'

'You know what I want, Perez. What I've always wanted. *You!*'

'Don't start that again, Elena. This time you'd better behave yourself. If you've agreed to come on this trip because of me, you'll be coming for the wrong reason.'

She flounced away, and Perez followed her. He didn't like the woman; but, even so, his eyes were drawn to the swing of her sensual hips. She had a great body, and his imagination teased him as he enjoyed the sight.

But he knew that what he and Elena had enjoyed in the past had been pure lust, not love. Animal passion was no longer the only thing Perez was looking for. Putting thoughts of everything irrelevant out of his mind, he shook hands with the fat Greek. He wanted to get the meeting over with as soon as possible. Whatever else Sinon was up to that sultry evening was none of his business.

All Perez had to think about now was the crazy little rich girl he was being paid to take into the Xingu. She apparently had a death-wish, and it was up to him to see that she didn't get hurt. And he intended to do just that. However much it annoyed him.

'Perez? Yes, I think I've heard of him. Come on, Dad, what's the mystery?' Gina could tell by the tone of his voice over the phone that something wasn't right.

'There's no mystery,' came the short reply.

Gina grinned. She knew her father better than that, and she was intrigued. 'Not much there isn't! Is this Perez a problem?'

There was a moment's silence, then, 'No, no problem. But he's an unusual man. I just want you to be aware of it, that's all.'

'Sounds marvellous!'

'Gina!'

'Okay, Dad, I'm aware. Don't worry, I can handle a guide – unusual or not!'

'I sincerely hope so.' He rang off.

Gina spent the rest of the afternoon completing her plans. She'd worked for this trip for months, and nothing was going to stop her now. And as she lay sprawled on the floor with her lists scattered all around, her excitement rose. She had no idea why she should be so compulsively attracted to the thousands of miles of Brazilian interior, but something was driving her toward it; something was telling her that she must write about the forest – photograph it, make some kind of pictorial gesture before the human species spoiled it all.

She sat back on her heels, her lips pursed thoughtfully. She had made another decision the night before. However much she loved her father, she was finished with the company. She had no longer any wish to be associated with anything that was harmful to the Amazon!

Later, she took a shower. Throwing on a light robe, she wandered from room to room, watering the array of house-plants. She had reminded Maria about it many times, but the girl didn't seem to listen. Not that she could blame her. Their house girl had far more important things to do than worry about Gina's pampered plants. She had Manuel to take care of, for one thing, and five growing kids. Plants could wait.

It was not easy to survive here when your husband had been hurt in an accident and your two young sons were forced out of school to take his place. And netting food in the Para was no pleasant afternoon's fishing on a riverbank! It was a matter of survival or starvation!

Gina glanced up as the doorbell rang. Spying through the blinds, she saw Mark Baxter waiting on the veranda. Damn! She didn't want to see him again so soon! But it was no good pretending she was out, because her car was standing in the drive.

'I had to see you,' Mark said as she let him in. 'Your father tells me you're off on a trip.'

'That's right.' She felt extremely annoyed as he followed her into the cool, tree-shaded yard at the back of the house, where a small grove of rubber trees was planted to withstand the onslaught of a tropical climate of hot sun and lashing storms. 'Drink?' She was trying to be polite.

'Please.'

She went into the kitchen and poured iced tea into two tall glasses. When she came back, he was sitting down, flipping through a magazine. He looked up. 'Gina, I think you know why I'm here.'

'I hope it's to apologise for that stupid letter.' She couldn't help herself. She had to let him know that his behaviour had been abominable.

'I don't want you to go, Gina!

She stared back at him. 'Just where don't you want me to go?' Her tone was acid.

'The Xingu's no place for a girl'

She saw red. 'How dare you tell me what to do!' she snapped. 'Just go away!'

'No matter what you say or do, I still care for you.' He was determined to stand his ground. 'I'm concerned for your safety. You don't understand what the forests are like.'

'That's exactly the point. I will soon enough.' She was becoming angrier every minute.

'You're risking your life! What for? Shots of a few dumb creatures? Indians? Miles of trees?'

His scathing indictment of her lifetime ambition made her stomach tighten. Not a muscle of her face moved, but her blue eyes hardened. 'Nothing is going to stop me now. I'm going into the Xingu!'

'Then you're crazy!' Mark shook his head desperately.

'So I've been told.' She looked into his pale, drawn face and shrugged her indifference. How could she get through to him that she didn't want him – and that she wanted the Xingu? If only he would go away and leave her in peace.

She tried again. If she was reasonable, he might. 'Look, Mark, I'm not stupid. Nor am I looking at the interior through rose-coloured glasses. I'm fully aware of the dangers. But it's something I have to do. And, anyway, my dad wouldn't let me go out there alone. He's found me a good guide. Perez.'

'Perez!' The venom in his voice shook her a little.

'You know him?'

'For God's sake, Gina. Don't go with him, please!'

'It's all arranged.' Her voice was firm. Mark cursed under his breath. 'What's the matter with him anyway?'

'I can't tell you, but if you insist on going, then watch your back!'

Gina had never seen Mark this fired up before. He jumped out of his chair, was about to stalk off, then swung round again to face her. His knuckles stood out white against the skin as he grasped the wooden rail of the balcony. She could see the angry flush beneath his sallow tan. He glared at her, as if he was seeing her for the very first time.

'You've really made up your mind?' he growled.

'Yes.'

'And there's nothing I can say to stop you?'

'Nothing!'

'Don't say you haven't been warned!' His face twisted with emotion.

'I think you should go, Mark,' Gina shrugged.

She had never seen such an expression on his face before, and she was relieved and delighted to show him out. She watched as he drove away, taking his anger out on the company Mercedes, like a spoiled child when he couldn't get what he wanted.

Gina went back inside to finish her tea. Sitting quietly to calm her nerves, she sipped its cold sweetness and wondered. Were they all victims of the unremitting heat? What kind of madness made people feel so strongly over here? She wondered too what it was that Perez had done to Mark to make him hate him so much.

3

As Perez drove away from the dockside and uptown, he was reasonably pleased with the way the meeting had gone, and even more pleased to have left the Paradiso.

Slowing down in the traffic, through the choke of diesel fumes he looked across at the huge complex of steel and glass that made up Baxter-Weber Incorporated. Its lights must cost a fortune in electricity, he thought. But it could afford anything it wanted. The company's fortunes had grown out of rubber. But there had been other dealings, too, and Perez was convinced that not all of them would stand up to too close a scrutiny.

He thought of the girl he was taking. Shaking his head, he pushed on the radio button. They had told him she wanted material for a book. But she wasn't a photographer by profession; she was probably executive fodder if they were willing to pay so much.

So why choose the Xingu? Was she another do-gooder? Another so-called intellectual who thought she could prevent the destruction by taking a few pictures?

Had they told her what dangerous territory the Xingu was? It puzzled him; but, on the other hand, he wasn't complaining. They'd met his fee without contention.

He'd take her into the Xingu if that's what she wanted! But, all the same, she'd be far better off staying put – safe and sound within the air-conditioned environs of her comfortable

Belem home.

He swore softly, impatiently flicking through the radio's frequencies. He wasn't impressed by anything that came out of Baxter-Weber.

And the trouble with some of these rich trendies was that they looked on a trip into the rainforest as a source of conscience regeneration. He hated the business world, with its love of money and material things. Every man had his price, Perez knew that. But the money he earned only served to give him the freedom he needed; to get where he wanted, away from civilisation and back to the cleanliness of the forests.

Even through the polluted haze, his nostrils picked up the sweet scents of flowers and herbs as he wound the window further down. He hated the city but loved the people in it. And he loved the great Para river that the city was built upon. The Para looked docile enough in the dark now as it lapped the embankment below, but it would soon show its teeth further on, when it rushed into the even greater one, the Amazon – O Rio Mar – the River Sea.

He moved on through the traffic, which never let up, even at midnight, listening to the sounds of the street traders still selling their wares, their calls mingling with the interminably raucous city sounds. He watched the *brejeiros* – the streetwise urchins – hustling for a meal; the fat cats in their limos; the floozies at their windows.

Here and there were orchid sellers, and his eyes lingered on one now, a kid of five or six, pushing his fragile merchandise into the arms of a tourist too drunk and weary to say no. Perez grinned ruefully. He hoped the blooms would last out the night.

Weaving in and out of the traffic, it seemed that the great throb of the South American continent pulsed beneath him, breathing life. Perez glanced at his watch as he turned into the drive of the flat he rented when he wasn't away on trips. Who the hell was waiting from him at this time of night? Then he recognised the company Mercedes. He grimaced as the tall man, dressed in a white suit, got out. His instincts had been proved right.

'*You!* What the hell are *you* doing here?' snarled Perez.

Mark Baxter had worked out his patter on the way over, but now that he faced Perez, he suddenly wanted a whisky to give him the courage, as he was conscious of the sweat along his upper lip.

'This isn't a social call, Perez.'

Perez glared at him. 'I'm pleased to hear it! Now, say what you have to say and get the hell out of here! I want to get to bed.' He couldn't stand Baxter after what he'd done, depriving him of the only girl he'd loved.

'You're taking a girl on a hike. For the company.' Mark wasn't going to stay a minute more than he needed.

'Don't tell me she's something to do with you?' retorted Perez.

'She means a great deal to me! I want to make sure she'll be safe – that you'll look after her ...' Mark faltered.

'You've a nerve!' Perez tried to rein in his temper. If he hadn't, he'd have floored him. 'You dare ask me that, after what you did to Dorita? You could have saved her. You could have pulled her out of the river. But you stood there, shaking!' Perez accused contemptuously, his tone more hostile now. 'You're taking a big chance coming here tonight, Baxter. I pity the girl, if she's mixed up with you.'

Mark backed away as Perez stepped nearer – he had sampled Perez's anger before. Next moment, Perez was thrusting his face into his. 'I'll take as much care of her as I would any client. But I can't say that your coming here tonight has endeared her to me! Anyway, I assure you that your girlfriend will be in better hands than Dorita was. Now, get out of here before I break your neck.'

Mark needed no second telling. Perez's eyes narrowed as he jumped back into the car and slammed the door. A second later, the Mercedes' tyres were screaming through the dust, carrying him back into the hole he'd crawled out of.

Perez groaned, lifted his eyes to the black night sky and

cursed himself for his weakness. Would he ever come to terms with Dorita's death?

The freighter's black bulk towered above the dockside. She was filthy, her hull showing streaks of rust. There was a green coat of weed along her waterline, layered with the silt and river effluence that had gathered as she'd chugged up the Para to the city of Belem.

Tied up in the big ship's shadow was a dug-out canoe, and in it, sleeping soundly, lay four young Indian boys. Now and then, one would stir as the night wind rocked the canoe, or when disturbed by a shout from a nearby bar as a seaman came stumbling out, his unsteady arms groping around his even more unsteady woman.

On the dockside, the bright lights of the Paradiso Bar still beckoned. It was near to 4.00 in the morning, but the place was still full of European sailors hell-bent on enjoying themselves now that their cargoes of rubber and green bananas had been loaded.

A few local girls, weary faced, barely out of childhood, were their company. They looked older than their years in their tight, bright skirts and bandeaux-covered breasts. They lived on the edge of an unwise economy and earned their living the only way they could, selling themselves for a few *cruzeiros* – or a few grams of dope.

Everywhere was the sour smell of unwashed bodies and stale food; but, still sitting at the bar, looking dangerously out of place, was Elena, her opulent European elegance sharply contrasting with that of the poor bargirls.

Sinon, who had been drinking heavily, was seated nearby, ensconced in a quiet conversation with the Indian chief, Santana. The Greek's suit was expensive and his fingers were loaded with rings. Like Elena, he looked totally out of place in the forlorn surroundings. Yet the locals recognised the two as frequent customers, who could often be found there in the middle of the night.

Elena tipped her glass to allow the fiery liquid to touch her tongue before it flashed down her throat. Sinon winked and gestured for Diego to refill his glass. The Portuguese owner hurried forward to comply; he did not wish for Senhor Sinon's anger that night. No more police. There was too much at stake.

The sailors shouted noisily, roaring for more spirits to slake their unrestricted thirsts. They were singing their drinking songs now. They had hardly noticed when the Indian had first walked in. The locals ignored him, but were conscious of his presence.

Elena regarded Sinon and Santana indifferently. Her lover was an expert at deceit. His name suited him; Sinon, *the deceiver*. The name of the Greek who had tricked the Trojans with the great wooden horse. She continued to sip her drink. Sinon was an expert on horses, too; but his expertise stopped with the glossy darlings of the racetrack. Such a pastime involved a lot of money, and he had plenty of that! He kept her content enough with a constant supply of expensive clothes and jewellery. These things were necessary for Elena – her life-support system. More necessary to her than the air she breathed.

She turned her attention away from her companion. Only one thing was on her mind. Getting Perez back. It was the only attraction of making another boring, uncomfortable trek into the interior; but it wouldn't be so easy this time! Before, he had been missing his pretty little native girl, but now … Elena's boredom was suddenly replaced by excitement at the thought of the two of them together. She looked up, smiling as Diego refilled her glass again and again ...

On the waterfront, his business with Sinon finished, Santana was making silent gestures to the boys. They were awake now and propelling the dug-out toward their chief. As the canoe reached him, Santana sprang into it. The boys paddled urgently, heading out toward the middle of the Para. Then the river mist surrounded them, enveloping the tiny boat, and soon its presence was lost in the darkness of the river.

Finally, the lights of Diego's bar went out as the last of the drunken sailors stumbled back toward his freighter and the cab carrying Sinon and his girlfriend nosed its way through the traffic toward the smartest district in Belem.

Perez's first glimpse of Mark Baxter's girl came as she stepped off the company aircraft that had brought her to Cachimbo. Gina Matheson moved easily, with a very expensive-looking camera slung across her shoulder, and her air of confidence was contagious. As she looked round – doubtless for him – the slim, tanned blonde in the flatteringly simple white dress seemed a mixture of waif and woman, reminding him of a shy young doe.

But at that moment Perez had no time to speculate on anything, especially about a girl who belonged to Baxter. He was far too busy seeing that the Indian boys were getting the gear properly loaded in the back of the truck.

But the next brief glance had a strange effect on him. Perez suddenly found that he couldn't take his eyes off her. A second later, he decided that he was paid to be polite and he ought to make himself known. And quickly. He strode over. Then she was smiling, putting out her hand; and when she spoke, her English was perfect, without a trace of an accent.

'Mr Perez? I'm Gina Matheson.'

'Miss Matheson.' His voice was mellow. It was stupid but, at that moment, Gina wondered if he could sing, given the depth of his chest. Not that she was an opera fan! He also had the build for it. He was very tall. He must have been at least six-four, because he towered over her. Suddenly she felt small and helpless, wondering what it would like to be crushed close to his body and carried struggling like Scarlett O'Hara up to bed. She blinked and swallowed. What was happening?

And Perez was still staring into her eyes as if he'd never seen a woman before. She had to say something, instead of just standing there, her insides turning over at what she was thinking. To combat her confusion, she looked around.

'So this is Cachimbo.' She hoped that her voice didn't sound as weak as her knees.

He'd been totally surprised by the deep blue of her eyes, fringed strangely with luxurious black lashes. And she was looking up at him from under them in a most disconcerting way. Perez's sudden defence was to quip, 'I sincerely hope so, Miss Matheson, since that was your destination.'

Gina caught her breath at the mockery in his tone. She came back to herself swiftly. This was no time for sexual fantasy. She had to stop it! 'A guide with a sense of humour,' she returned.

'You need one down here, I can tell you,' he replied.

For a wary moment, the two sized each other up. Gina had been quite curious about the man who was going to take her on the most dangerous journey of her life. From the way he looked at her, she was clearly not what he had been expecting! But then, he wasn't what she'd imagined him to be either!

Wow, what a face! she thought, going off again. It was dominated by eyes with dark, wonderful wide pupils, which lingered as they casually looked her up and down. Perez's hair was long, and curled over the collar of his khaki bush jacket. She thought briefly about Mark's near-shaven skull and tossed the comparison away forever.

She laughed softly. 'What's the matter, Mr Perez? You look surprised!'

Perez frowned, thinking he hadn't seen such blue eyes since he left England. Then he snapped out of it and shrugged. 'Little surprises me, Miss Matheson, but I didn't realise you were English.'

'Didn't you? Matheson is an English enough name.'

'I suppose it is.' He'd never thought about her surname, only that she had something to do with Baxter-Weber.

'What did you think I was?'

'German.'

'Why?'

He shrugged. 'Who knows? Come on, the others are over here.' He led her toward the truck where Sinon and Elena waited.

As they approached, the Greek's bloated face was already

weighing up Gina's undoubted charms, and his dark, frog-like eyes narrowed in interested speculation. 'Welcome to Cachimbo, Miss Matheson,' he said, as Gina shook his hand. It was cold and clammy, and she withdrew her fingers quickly.

'Thank you, Mr Demetrios.' Then Gina smiled at the girl who'd come along to keep her company. 'Elena?' She was rewarded with only a brief nod. Thinking that the girl had no need to be so rude, and wondering why, Gina decided to ignore her, but not before she'd taken a good look at someone she feared was going to be a pretty useless confidante.

The Greek girl was extremely good-looking, with a penchant for expensive clothes. Her jeans were designer, and her legs seemed to go on forever. Her shirt was of raw silk, and the thin material exposed the fact she wasn't wearing a bra. She also exuded the kind of animal hostility that only one woman can have for another. Most incongruous were her exquisite painted nails.

Where on earth had Perez found his two companions? They looked more like types to be found in a nightclub in Brasilia or Rio, rather than a couple ready for a trek in the forests. This wasn't what her father had meant when he had said he wasn't going to let his daughter go off into the jungle with a 'a parcel of men.' But then she came round. So if the girl wanted to be rude, she'd be rude back. But before it came to that, she'd try once more to be civil.

Elena remained motionless, watching Gina's every move, until Perez shouted, 'Elena, get in the truck instead of lazing about over there.'

Gina lifted her eyebrows. He'd better not be rude to her like that! But the response his command elicited from Elena was anything but anger. The girl stretched herself sinuously, shot a mocking glance at him from narrowed dark eyes, and with a tiny shrug of the shoulders, gracefully climbed aboard.

Any woman would have recognised her response. It was blatantly obvious. Gina's quick eyes had already summed up that there had been, or there still was, some kind of relationship between Elena and Perez.

That the man was attractive was as clear as day. Gina was pretty sure that he must have a reputation with women. She herself had felt his sensuality the moment he'd taken her hand. And had succumbed to it. Which was not a good sign. She wanted no dangerous liaisons. She was off men. And ones like him in particular, although she had to admit she'd never met one before. Just thinking about it made her toes curl!

When her father had called him unusual, she'd made some inquiries. Most of them had drawn a blank. Perez was evidently an enigma where his personal life was concerned. All she'd gleaned was that he did his work extremely well and then took off into the forests again; that he'd never been seen in any English club, although he was half English; that he lived hard and wasn't keen on European women. So where did Elena fit in? Gina's brow crinkled.

In fact, one of the older company wives, whose executive husband had been on a trip led by Perez, had told her, tongue-in-cheek, 'I'd watch him, if I were you, Gina. Jack says he's the worst kind. Devastatingly handsome, and arrogant about being so good at his job.' Then she'd grinned ruefully and added, 'Lucky old you. I wish I was coming. Maybe *you'll* find out what makes him tick.'

Yes, Perez was a man who looked like he'd take a woman in and then walk away without a second glance; he was certainly a man to be wary of. But maybe she would find his weakness. That was, *if* she took him on!

He was staring at her again. 'Ready?' he asked, his eyebrows indicating the truck's cab.

'Almost, but I'd like to get a shot of our truck first.' She slipped her camera off her shoulder. He was frowning. 'After all, that's what I'm here for,' she added lightly. He shrugged and began to walk away. 'Oh, no, I'd like *you* in it,' she said. 'And the Indians. Do *they* like having their pictures taken?'

'More than I do!' Perez growled. He looked up at the back of the truck and beckoned. 'Caninde! Jeronimo! Get down here and have your photo taken!' Gina could have laughed out loud at the uncomfortable look on Perez's face.

'Thank you. Over there,' she nodded. She caught a glimpse of Sinon Demetrios slipping round the back of the vehicle. He evidently didn't want to be in the picture – and she was glad.

Next moment, she was squaring up the three of them in her viewfinder. She smiled involuntarily at how Perez's muscular bulk dwarfed the tiny Indians, who were grinning happily. But he was scowling now. 'Do you think you could look a bit happier, Mr Perez?' she called, enjoying it immensely. She couldn't catch what he said.

Seconds later, her eyes were travelling slowly down his magnificent body. They lingered on his open shirt, which revealed a luxurious mass of chest hair and caressed his bronzed, smooth skin, which seemed to have been carved from a teak tree. They swept on lower and lower, below his intricately carved wide leather belt toward his crotch …

'Miss Matheson, will you get on with it,' he snarled.

'Sorry,' she lied, 'I was just finding the exact position.' She was sure that she'd been rumbled, because as she pressed the trigger, she caught a sardonic half-smile, which twisted his fine lips. 'Excellent,' she murmured to herself, moistening her own lips with her tongue. 'Okay. Thanks, it's great,' she called as she reviewed the picture. 'Would you like to see?'

'No, thanks!' Next moment, Perez was dismissing the Indians, who leapt into the back of the truck. As she approached, he came over to meet her. 'Don't think I didn't know what you were up to,' he said quietly.

Her eyes widened. 'What do you mean?'

'Two can play at that game. I'll show you and your camera a lot more interesting sights than me. Things you can get your teeth into.'

She was suddenly taken aback by the power in his voice; by his maleness. 'Is that a threat?' she countered.

'No, it's a promise,' he breathed, his golden voice changing into dark, runny honey, which was seeping through her bones.

'Good,' she said. 'After all, that's what I'm here for.'

She felt her face and her body glowing at the brief encounter. It was then that the fat bulk of Sinon reappeared, and she was aware of Elena's surly face glowering at her from the driver's cab. And that electrifying moment of contact dissipated like morning mist from the treetop canopy.

A few moments later, Gina shrugged inwardly as the truck jolted her bones uncomfortably, and the ill-assorted quartet rumbled off along the narrow road. No-one appeared to be speaking to anyone, even though they were in such close contact.

Elena had made sure she was sitting next to Perez, who was driving. Sinon was next to Gina, and his leg had a disgusting habit of pressing itself against hers. At one point, she had a sudden desire to stab it with the small pair of scissors that she was carrying in her holdall, but instead she willed herself to keep calm. They'd soon be at the first stop, and afterwards she'd make it clear that she didn't want to be sitting by Sinon again. After all, she was paying.

If Elena had a problem with her, so what? The dislike was mutual. And Gina wasn't worried about Perez's effect on herself! Why should she be? In fact, she'd enjoyed taking him on. As much as when she'd looked at him through the camera's lens! Besides, it added a little more to a trek that she expected to be nothing but excitement all the way.

Anyway, who cared about Perez and his relationship with a woman? Not Gina. She was far too engrossed on her trip of a lifetime. She confessed to herself that she'd rather have been sitting next to him, though. His leg pressing against hers would have been infinitely preferable to Sinon's. In fact, the idea made her sweat even more. It was so damned hot! She moistened her lips again with the bottle of water she was carrying, and told herself bravely that she wasn't going to worry about trivialities.

But by the time they reached the stop-over house, a weary Gina had thought better of her initial reaction to Perez. All those wild imaginings of hers were quite ridiculous. She'd probably been playing with fire. He'd looked extremely put out having his picture taken. And he hadn't had a word to say to any of them since. She'd probably offended him.

She had to remember he was her guide, and she told herself

sternly that she had better take notice of him – and not only for her father's sake! She had to spend the next three months of her life with this man. Dangerous months in a dangerous place. And Gina wanted to go on living. There was no doubt about that!

4

The room Gina was forced to share with Elena was functional. There were no luxuries, and she had expected none. 'Which bed do you prefer, Elena?' she asked, once they were alone. 'This one,' she indicated to the bed nearest the window, 'or that?' Her question was answered by a shrug.

Gina got the message. If she'd even remotely believed that the girl might be her friend, then she might as well forget it. She threw her case on the bed by the door, unpacked a change of clothes and took off her white dress. It had always been a favourite with her, but now the humidity had turned it into a damp mass of wilted fabric, which she was glad to be free of.

Wrapped in a robe, she went out along the passage, stepping gingerly along the creaking floorboards until she found the shower. It creaked ominously when she turned it on, and for a good three minutes the water that came gushing from the spray was the colour of earth.

A little later, when Gina went back into the bedroom, the other girl was seated in a cane chair polishing her nails. From outside came the strange sounds of unfamiliar birds. Sighing, she tried again. 'The bathroom's an experience, Elena, but it's better than none, I suppose. Have you tried it?'

The girl shrugged. 'I bathed this morning.' She looked up, her almond-shaped eyes glittering her hostility. 'If you are trying to make yourself attractive for Perez, you can forget it.

He's a man not easily fooled by womanly charms. He isn't keen on English girls!'

'Are you trying to warn me off?' asked Gina cuttingly.

'If you like.' Elena raised a hand dismissively. 'Perez and I have an understanding. Perhaps if you have ideas for yourself, you'd better ask him about us.'

'Perhaps I would, if I was interested enough,' Gina retorted.

Elena got up and went over to the set of drawers that served as a dressing table. Her movement was graceful and, even though Gina already had enough reason to dislike the woman, she had to admit to her undeniable beauty.

The two girls didn't speak again. Gina lay down on her bed, wondering what the hell she'd let herself in for. She pursed her lips. What a situation! Here she was, in the back of beyond, sharing a room with a girl who despised her, and her life in the hands of the most attractive man she had ever seen.

The plane journey and the unbearable heat began to take their toll. Soon Gina became drowsy, and she was almost asleep when a knock on the door roused her. The door opened briefly. It was Perez. 'Better get dressed. We're meeting downstairs in two minutes.'

'Who's we?' Gina raised her weary head.

'All of us. That's if you still want to go into the Xingu!' He nodded toward Elena's slumbering form. 'It doesn't matter about her. Let her finish her beauty sleep.'

'Are you sure?'

'I said leave her.'

'Right.'

Gina dressed quickly and joined them. Sinon was there already.

'Come, Gina, sit by me. Drink?'

'Iced water, please.'

'You'll be lucky. Out here, spirits come easier.' The Greek laughed.

'Then nothing, thanks.'

'I've bottled water in the truck,' Perez said shortly, coming in. 'I'll go and get it. No ice, though.' He disappeared again.

'What's the meeting about?' she asked.

'To tell us his plans. And to warn you.'

'Why?'

'It's only a ritual. Perez likes to put the fear of God in us.'

Perez returned with the water, then unrolled a map. 'This is where we are now,' he pointed, 'and this is where the highway starts.'

For the first time, Gina noticed the twisted band of carved beads around Perez's muscular wrist, and she wondered how he had come by it.

Perez caught her glance. The band was a token he prized. He had been given it when he had saved the life of the son of a chief. Besides, he was playing safe. Superstition held that it guaranteed a man's strength.

Sinon yawned and mopped his face with a soiled handkerchief, as Perez pointed to another spot on the map. 'This is where it's most dangerous.'

'Where?' Gina asked. She leaned forward, and Perez's nearness made the air sizzle.

'Everywhere is in the Xingu, but this place in particular,' he answered dryly. 'There's still time to turn back.'

'No!'

'You're sure?'

'I'm sure! I'm here and here to stay,' she retorted.

'Very well. We leave the truck here. After that, we continue on foot. It won't be very comfortable.' His eyes raked her body. 'I'm glad to see you're out of that dress.'

'Why?' She frowned.

'It was very pretty but, unfortunately, it wouldn't have protected you from marauding leeches.'

'Are you trying to be rude?' she flashed. 'I wore that dress because I like it, and it was comfortable to travel in. Don't worry, Mr Perez, I have the *right* clothes with me. As for the trek being uncomfortable, I never expected it to be anything else.'

'Okay, okay,' replied Perez annoyingly. 'I was only trying to be helpful. In any case …' his eyes were raking over her again, '… I liked it too.'

'Thank you,' snapped Gina. At that moment, Perez stared at her as if he knew what she looked like without anything on at all. Suddenly she felt hot and angry. She glanced at his moody face as he returned his attention to the map, and knew he was already looking on her as some terrible liability.

'We go tomorrow,' concluded Perez, folding the map and getting to his feet. 'Tonight, I suggest you get plenty of sleep. It will be the last decent bed you'll lie on for yonks.'

'Right,' she said, wondering what indecent bed he'd been sharing lately.

'Make sure you check everything. If you do forget something, we can't come back for it.' He was treating her like a child.

'You don't have to spell it out,' she said. 'I'll let Elena know what you've said.'

'She already does,' said Sinon, pouring out a large brandy. 'Anyway, knowing Elena, she'll probably stay at the settlement. The Xingu isn't exactly her idea of a vacation.'

Gina stopped in her tracks, his words sinking in. Suddenly she realised that there was a strong possibility that she would be alone in the rainforests with no-one but Perez and the Greek. 'Elena will be staying?'

'She'll do as she damn well likes,' the Greek chuckled. 'But she's used to it.'

'My father's paid a lot of money for this trip,' she reminded him coldly. 'According to him, Elena is part of the deal. She'll do what I tell her. And so will you, if you know what's good for you!'

Perez grinned as Sinon shrugged.

Gina turned to Perez. 'Good night, Mr Perez.'

'Goodnight, Miss Matheson.'

Gina ran up the few stairs. She mustn't quarrel with Perez. He was the only one who could get her in and out of the Xingu in one piece. Later, she went out on to the small veranda, feeling a million miles from anything she had ever known before. The moon rode low and a breeze stirred. It was a pity to end the evening on so sour a note, and on so beautiful a night.

Then a shadowy figure appeared beside her. 'Nothing quite compares to the stars in the tropics.'

Gina looked up into Perez's eyes. Above them the vast dark sky was silent. 'Nothing,' she replied.

'Beautiful as this night is, Miss Matheson, it would be better to sleep. Tomorrow will be hard.'

She glanced up, and her eyes met his. The fickle moon was lighting his face, and for one brief moment the world faded. A shudder ran through her.

'Goodnight again,' he said.

'Goodnight.'

Then he was gone. But in spite of what he'd said, Gina couldn't sleep. She tossed and turned, remembering ruefully those confident words to her father just a few days ago. *I can handle a guide!* My God! Could she handle one like Perez?

5

'Wake up!'

Sinon blinked open a puffy lid before turning on his back and rubbing his eyes with the tips of his soft white fingers. 'Go to hell, Perez!' he replied.

'Suit yourself, but I'm leaving on time, whether you're ready or not. We need to be at least half-way to the settlement by nightfall.'

'I'll make it, don't worry. This trip's important to me too, remember.' He turned over again.

Perez frowned. He remembered all right. He got up and looked through the window. Already the street was alive. A dust cloud hung over it, shrouding everything in a fine red mist. And, as a big refrigerated truck thundered by, it threw up even more. Perez watched the activity below him. Cachimbo had started life humbly as an airstrip; as nothing more than a stepping-stone into the profitable interior. But now it was growing, spreading its wings.

The main street was wide, even by Brazilian standards; yet, even so, the congestion of vehicles and lumber-laden mule carts was already causing a jam as they jostled for space. Traders were loading the guavas and green bananas into trucks, preparing for their trade along the river. Groups of loggers and miners, boisterous and arguing in a haze of cheap cigarillo smoke, were heaving themselves into the waiting trucks before setting out for the forest.

They contrasted sharply with the silent line of Indian women who were passing below him now. The baskets on their backs were empty. When they returned home that night, they would have filled them a hundred times or more with their daily quota of the coffee crop.

Leaving Sinon where he was, Perez went downstairs. He still had work to do of his own. He swallowed a cup of hot, bitter coffee and then went out to the vehicles.

Caninde and Jeronimo, his Indian mechanics, were good, but he took nothing for granted. It wouldn't do to break down in the forest. He checked out the engine of the supply truck while the Indians worked on the Toyota. When he was satisfied, Perez drove the truck into the side street ready to load.

Sitting moodily at the wheel, he wiped down the windscreen and watched Gina Matheson emerge from the building. Her movements were graceful even at this early hour, intensifying a long-stilled ache in his flesh. She had tied her blonde hair back in a bandeau, and her grey shorts and faded green top were not only practical, but they also hugged the tops of her long, golden legs – giving Perez ideas he hadn't had for a long time.

He turned away. She smiled as she climbed in beside him, greeting him with a flash of white teeth and an air of exuberant freshness. 'All set?'

'Almost.' Perez turned to look at her. She seemed edgy this morning, talking for the sake of it. He wasn't really listening to what she was saying. He could smell her scent, and was too conscious of the hot feeling in his gut. *He wanted to touch her.*

A strange kind of emotion caught at his throat, and he thought what a waste a girl like Gina Matheson would be on an idiot like Baxter. He turned away purposely, watching the two Indians tease the local girls as they passed by. He took in the girls' happy faces and lissom figures; their graceful necks adorned with beads. They reminded him of Dorita, sweet and uncomplicated. He'd known too many women. Now only the forest held his trust.

Excusing himself, Perez jumped out of the Toyota to oversee the loading. He needed to move about, to think about the trip, and to lose body contact with Gina. He assumed his usual self-contained character. There was no room for sex – nor sentiment – where they were going.

A soft, pasty hand gripped his sleeve. 'How long before we leave?'

Perez glared down at Sinon. 'Five minutes – if you can stay awake that long! Make yourself useful and give Caninde a hand.'

Sinon shrugged and shuffled off toward the Indian. Watching him, Perez humped a sack of rice over to the other truck. He wished Sinon wasn't coming – nor his girlfriend! He neither liked nor trusted either of the Greeks; but the man was too useful to leave behind, and where he went, so did Elena. He would have to put up with their devious ways for a few weeks more. He only hoped it would be worth it.

Feeling less than useless, Gina climbed out of the Toyota too, offering to help the drivers with the loading. They seemed embarrassed by her offer, and Perez explained that, to an Indian, such work was for men. Women had another role – they were expected to know their place.

Gina chose to ignore this and handed them the gear with quick, impatient movements. She had to do something! Besides, the actions were helping to bring her back to reality, her brain unwilling to admit the momentary weakness she felt whenever Perez was near.

She could feel even now how close he was, but she didn't dare to look at him again – not until she had her wayward feelings back under firm control.

It was already two o'clock by the time they were ready to move, and Elena finally made her appearance. Clutching a small overnight bag, she looked more equipped for a day at the races than the long hard trek! As she wriggled herself into the seat next to Perez, he threw Gina a quick, searching glance. He had thought this might happen, and wondered if Gina would complain. After all, her father was footing the bill and, he reasoned, she had the right to demand the most comfort.

She didn't complain. She retuned his glance with a brief,

perceptive stare and turned away quickly, climbing into the back with Sinon. Perez admired her composure but didn't fancy the idea of her stuck in the back with the Greek for the long hours before they reached the settlement.

'Just a temporary arrangement,' he told her as he got in beside Elena. 'I'll see you get the front seat soon!'

'Don't worry about me, I'm all right.' But, as they started off, Gina wondered if perhaps that was too optimistic a remark. Even now, she could smell Sinon's overwhelming body stench.

After a mere five miles, the inside of the Toyota was becoming unbearable. And the further they drove, the more Sinon sweated; but whether it was from the heat or from his constant brushing against her leg, Gina couldn't be sure.

Following the loaded truck and its two Indian drivers, they headed south toward the highway and, from there, on into the Xingu. Once out of the town, the track became potholed and narrow. Around them, Gina could see nothing but the vast dank chambers of the forest. It was as if the great hothouse of trees was closing in around her, their barks choking with the vines that entwined them. Occasionally, Perez pointed out orchids or a particular species of exotic bird. Four uncomfortable hours passed before they stopped, braking suddenly and halting on a high plateau.

Judging from the small scattering of empty Coca-Cola and beer cans, plus the abandoned wreck of an old Volkswagen, the clearing acted as a sort of campsite for any itinerant logger. It was unseen from the road, tucked away about a mile off the main track. And, untidy or not, the place was like paradise to Gina. She felt she'd been travelling forever; but when she glanced at the mileage dial, she saw that they'd done hardly a hundred miles – the pace was slow and punishing.

'We'll camp here tonight,' Perez told them.

With great relief, Gina climbed out, moving carefully so as not to awaken the sleeping Sinon. She breathed in deeply, taking long, gulping breaths of air. She felt hot and sticky, and longed for a cooling shower just then. She was already wilting from the strength-sapping atmosphere of the slumbering jungle.

Unseen creatures of the forest started a screaming babble of sound; a warning chorus to the strange ones in their midst. From the tiny clearing, the far-away sparkle of the river was in itself a spectacle, and craning her neck to look down, fatigued as she was, Gina suddenly felt she was witness to a miracle.

She walked to the edge of the clearing, where the canopy of trees thinned out. Then it suddenly started to rain. Great soaking drops came down in one heavy sheet. Then it stopped again just as abruptly; but not before it had turned the dry dust of the clearing into a mire of red mud. But Gina was still sweating, and as she moved further toward the water's sound, hoping for a breeze, she had to brush away swarms of flies.

She gasped at the sight below her: rapids beating at the rocks, spilling the water into a boiling mass of spume and foam until it reached the waiting river, lying hundreds of metres below. She swayed, dizziness overtaking her. She felt drowsy, asleep on her feet, until a steadying hand grabbed her shoulder.

'Careful,' Perez warned. 'They call this *el iman* – the magnet. The rapids can hypnotise – like a Svengali. The Indians say that the falls suck in a man's spirit and make him their own.'

'Thanks.' Gina stepped back, coming out of the daze. 'But it's so beautiful,' she said, her words lost in the cascade's thunder. 'The most spectacular thing I've ever seen!'

'This is only the beginning.' He was impressed by how sincere she sounded. 'Are you okay?'

Gina grinned. 'Yes, although I'm sore.'

Perez smiled 'Come on, you need a break.'

They rejoined the others. The Indians had set up an informal camp. A pan of rice was already being heated up on a primus stove, and a few small canvas stools had been brought out of the truck.

Perez handed her a can of beer, and she drank it gratefully. She sat down, watching the Indians as they prepared the food. 'Cold at nights,' explained Caninde. Pointing to her thin top, he added, 'You need more than that to sleep.'

'I'll remember. Thanks.'

Elena was lying lazily on a woollen rug, swiping at an insect that had settled on her skirt. She had pulled down her top, low enough almost to expose her breasts, and her skirt was hitched high over her hips. She was like a cat, feline, and sensually exuding the most direct and unrestricted sexual invitation Gina had ever seen.

Perez glowered. 'Cover up, Elena,' he ordered gruffly, glancing at the Indians. 'This isn't the poolside, and you ought to know better.'

The girl's vivid red lips curved in a wide smile that never reached her eyes. 'Whatever you say, Perez,' she purred.

Sinon, awake at last, was leaning against a boulder, puffing at a cigar, watching everything. Then he moved toward Elena and muttered something. He looked angry. Gina thought that Elena was probably the only one who could put up with his sweating, ugly body! Doubtless for a good reason!

'You eat now.' Jeronimo handed her a bowl. 'Is good – *mandioca* make lady strong.'

Thanking him, she looked down at the food. The grey mass of cassava plant and tinned fish certainly didn't look very appetising, but after one mouthful she found it was delicious, and, giving in to her hunger, she tucked in.

It was a sombre and silent party that shared the supper. Everyone seemed tired, except Perez, who despite the sweat stains along his back seemed unflagging in his constant checking of the trucks and stores.

Then they put up the tents and unloaded for the night. Gina's bones still hurt from the miles in the jolting Toyota, and she thought about her shower at home; of the soft, white towels; of her comfortable bed that would be unoccupied that night and for the next few weeks! She smiled, then sighed. There would be no comfortable beds for a long time. And the only showers would come from Mother Nature herself! Well, she'd asked for it. But, looking at the glum faces around her, she reflected that she had rather hoped for more pleasant company.

When supper was over, Gina wandered into the tent and rooted out a toilet bag from the depths of her holdall. She had decided to sponge herself down in the rushing stream that ran by the camp. Making sure she was entirely alone, she stripped off her clothes and waded into the clear, cold water. Perez was right! This was infinitely better than any shower at home. She wallowed for a time, then dried herself and, sitting on a fallen tree, stared up at the dramatic lianas writhing like ribbons around the trees.

'What's the matter?' asked Elena when Gina returned. 'Too much for you already?'

'No.'

'Do you wish you hadn't come?' she sneered.

'No.'

Elena eyed her slyly. 'I do,' she sighed, 'and you will too before long.'

'You're being well paid for the inconvenience,' snapped Gina.

Elena stared at her for a moment but didn't speak, then she looked away and picked a can from a box. 'Want another?' It was the first friendly sign the girl had shown.

'No. Thanks for asking, but I'm off to bed.'

'Suit yourself.'

'I will.'

Gina left the girl sitting alone with her beer and a cigarette. Once inside the tent, she checked her camera and wondered what the next day would bring. Then she took off her clothes, slipped into the sleeping bag and pulled over the mosquito net. Glancing at the luminous dial of her watch, she discovered it was almost midnight! She settled down, but through the open slit of the tent she could see Perez pacing around the clearing – a tall, lonely figure, rifle at his side.

The moon was up now like a great golden eye, and as Gina's eyes followed Perez, she thought how like the forest he was – alive, mysterious, vibrant – and almost frightening.

Perez opened his eyes, drowsy, still half asleep, his limbs cramped by the narrowness of the sleeping bag. Then he realised there was someone standing over him. Elena!

Gina woke up suddenly. Her eyes flicked across the tent, expecting to see Elena lying there, but the sleeping bag was empty. She turned onto her back, listening. What had disturbed her? Her watch said it was only 2.00 am. Then she recognised the voices of Perez and Elena. Looking out again, she saw that less than a hundred yards away, they stood together in the clearing. And she was snuggling up against him.

Gina closed the tent flap quickly. After all, their affair was nothing to do with her! But she felt extremely miserable and disappointed as she tried to go back to sleep.

Outside, Perez's arms came up abruptly, clamping on Elena's, which were clinging to him like a leech! He prised them off. 'Go to hell, Elena!' He strode off, leaving his one-time lover shaking with outrage and humiliation.

In the darkness of his tent, Sinon simmered with anger. *This time, Perez …* he whispered into the still darkness. *This time, Sinon is going to make you pay!*

When Elena returned to the tent, she glared down at Gina, who she knew was the only reason Perez didn't want her! As she climbed into her sleeping bag, she snarled under her breath, *You'll never have him. I'll see to that, little rich English mouse!*

6

Gina had already seen the highway from the air. Then it had reminded her of a long, orange-coloured zip stitched into the earth, that if someone was to pull open would split the dense jungle in two. From the ground, it was only a straight, featureless, dusty road, ochre-gravelled, with nothing to distinguish it from any other highway except for its borders of relentless, brooding forest and its incessant dawn chorus of shrieking howler monkeys.

Before packing up, they had breakfasted on fruit and water. And as three of the party had eaten, Perez and the Indians had co-ordinated in an impressive effort to stow away the camp. Soon they had been on their way, leaving every sign of their presence gone.

'How long will it take to reach the settlement?' Gina asked.

'Ten hours or so – we should make it by nightfall,' replied Perez.

Gina glanced at him, 'Barring any problems?'

Perez grinned. 'There'll be no problems.'

She thought it was a pity he didn't smile more often. She sighed, wondering what she could do about her sudden fascination with the man. His face was taut in the brightness of the sun's light, but he seemed less tense that morning, which she deduced was a result of a night's lovemaking with Elena. There was even a light-hearted flippancy in his tone as he added, 'Pass me the water?' She reached for the water bottle from the pocket of the door, unscrewing the cap and handing it to him. As he drank, Gina thought silently that if there was a flaw in his features at all, it was perhaps that his chin was a little too cleft.

Perez had insisted that Gina take the front seat that day, and Elena hadn't liked it at all. Since they'd started off, Gina had felt the Greek girl's glowering silence, broken now and again by Sinon's mocking laugh as she tried to protest. 'Come on, darling,' Sinon cajoled. 'We've been parted too long. Come and stay with old Sinon in the back while Miss Matheson entertains our guide.' Gina knew the girl didn't dare refuse Sinon, who was sitting with a fat hand twined in her black hair.

Gina glanced at her watch; it was three minutes past eight, and they'd already covered more than sixty miles. She looked out at the immense wilderness around them and then upwards at the speck of a white plane as it flew like a clumsy bird toward Cachimbo. In an effort to make conversation, she asked Perez, 'Do you miss England?'

'I never think about it. I can hardly remember my time over there.' He took a hand off the wheel and gestured toward the forest. 'I'd miss this too much. Here, humanity knows its place.'

She smiled. 'It's strange, isn't it?'

'Strange?'

'Yes. *Challenging!* Absorbing, dangerous, yet *intriguing!* I can understand how you love it. I do, as well.'

He glanced at her. 'Love? Is that how you see love – challenging, absorbing, intriguing and dangerous?'

'Don't you?'

He grinned, but afterwards, his face grew impassive. 'I don't look for love,' he commented quietly. They drove on for several minutes before he asked, 'What else do you *love?*'

Gina flashed, 'My father.'

'I don't know much about loving fathers – never having had one. Mine shipped me off to one of your English schools when I was too young to argue.' He sounded bitter. 'Maybe he thought it was best. I like to give him the benefit of the doubt.' He grinned wryly. 'Perhaps he hoped I wouldn't turn out to be like him!'

Gina smiled back, hoping to ease the tension that had suddenly sprung up within him. 'I didn't like school much either.'

They didn't speak again for a long while. All the time, she was remembering the night before, and the way he'd held Elena in his arms. They drove on in silence, broken only by the subdued sound of snoring from the back as Sinon slept again. They stopped only once – for lunch; more fruit and water.

Perez took this time to replenish the Toyota's tank from a petrol container in the second truck, and as he and Jeronimo checked out the vehicles, Gina grabbed the brief opportunity to stretch her aching muscles and to find out more about Caninde.

'Are you married, Caninde?' she asked as the Indian squatted on the ground.

He smiled, his brown skin reminding her of mahogany as he bit into a gourd. '*She* is my wife.' He pointed to the great forest behind them, and Gina knew that his remark was serious.

'But what about girls?'

He shrugged. 'Women are for the children and for the house. They are not for Caninde. They ask too much.'

She moved away, gaining what privacy she could from the trucks to answer the call of nature. Alone like this, she felt vulnerable. It was as if the jungle might encircle her and swallow her up, like a fly in some dark, immense web. Suddenly there was a cracking sound! Something whistled close to her ear as she scrambled up. Panicking, she looked round for Perez. Then he appeared from the undergrowth, rifle in hand.

'Okay?'

Anger flared in her eyes. 'You fired at me! What the hell do you think you're doing?'

Perez jerked his head to the ground; and, for the first time, she realised something was writhing in the undergrowth a yard or so from her. 'Looking after my interests. And I wouldn't have missed if I had been aiming at you. I asked if you were okay. Are you?'

'Yes.' She stared. 'Why?'

'A jiboa.' He picked up the creature with the butt of his rifle.

He hadn't aimed to kill, and as Gina stared at the hapless snake thrashing like a beautiful stream of sun-dappled water around the barrel's shaft, she realised how close she'd been to danger.

She inhaled deeply. The snake was easily ten or twelve feet long. The great creature of the forest was terrified now, and bent on getting away. Gina laughed nervously, 'How did you know it was there? Were you watching me?'

'Don't take it personally,' Perez returned, then tossed the reptile back into the undergrowth, 'but, yes, I was watching you. It's my job. Would you rather I didn't?' Without waiting for her answer, he turned on his heels and headed for the Toyota. She watched him go, her face red, then walked back to the truck, trying to look as if nothing had happened.

They continued on their journey. Further on, as they neared their destination, they passed a few Indians, most of them on foot. Here and there they straggled along the side of the road, crocodile-fashion, the men in front in their plaited straw headbands, shouldering their nets of *matrincha* fish, and the women and children following behind, naked and unadorned.

'Their way of life won't last much longer,' Perez remarked as they passed them. 'Their land's been damaged by Europeans. Their numbers are on the wane; but,' he added on a note of bitterness, 'we mustn't let a little thing like the Indians' way of life obstruct development, must we?'

Gina sighed. What Perez said was true, and her father's own company was a great deal to blame for it. Even travellers like their own little party were guilty, their very presence contributing to the Indians' decline. It had been hard enough for the natives to survive before the Europeans came. Disease, tribal wars, the desperately low birth rate had all played their part. And if roads and airstrips were pushed right through this wilderness – as, one day, they surely would be – then that would spell the inevitable end, as the culture of these simple people would disappear forever.

'We're almost at Santana's now,' Perez informed her as he

wrenched the Toyota off the highway and onto a side track, bringing her back to earth. 'You'll see the village in a minute.'

The vehicle swerved round the bend. They had made good time, as there was still three hours to go before sunset. The track narrowed, cutting a strand through the towering forest. Through the enveloping gloom, Gina could see the old lianas looping themselves around the trunks of dead trees, while new ones were already springing up to take their place. It reminded her of creation: the primeval swamp at the dawn of man.

Then, through the steaming darkness, Gina glimpsed a shaft of light, fleeting, silver and bright, like a flash of water. 'Are we near the river?'

'Not far. We're at one of the tributaries.' Perez braked hard over the uneven surface. 'It's hard going here; we have to take care not to get bogged down. Further on, this stretch turns into rapids before it merges into the Xingu river.'

Suddenly, they were out of the darkness and into the clearing. For one exciting moment, Gina stared at the cluster of haystack dwellings formed into a circle within a ragged compound. She sensed Perez's eyes on her as she looked toward the dark river and then turned back again, aiming her camera toward the women who squatting at their work outside the primitive houses.

She snapped away at the white patches of manioc flour at the women's feet and then at the women themselves, whose hands and arms were worn thin and sinewy by the constant pounding, grating and sifting of the raw, bitter cassava roots. 'What a hard life! Will they bother about my taking photographs?'

His dark eyes glittered. 'I should think they're used to it by now. And as for their hard life, they don't see it that way. In the language of the Indian, there is no word for work.'

Gina smiled down into the inquisitive faces of the women and noticed that, of the men remaining in the village, most were old. The younger ones, Perez explained, would be off to the forest to hunt; or to the river to fish. He broke off as a half dozen or so of the villagers came up to them and surrounded the

Toyota. Then Gina suddenly found herself being welcomed by the descendants of the once-dreaded head-hunting tribe of the Chavante Indians.

'Nervous?'

Gina glanced quickly into Perez's amused face. 'No.'

He laughed, opening the Toyota's door. 'I'm pleased to hear it. Come on, I'll introduce you.'

As the four of them climbed out, Perez spoke fluently in the Indian dialect – a strange sound to Gina's unaccustomed ears. Once the long ritual of greeting was done with, a courteous and kindly Indian led them over to another of the dwellings; a palm-thatched *maloca*, set square in the centre of the commune, and bigger than the rest.

'They call this the House of Strangers,' Perez translated. 'Apparently we're honoured. They tell me it's been built specially for us; although,' he grinned, 'I rather doubt it.' He appraised her upturned face. 'Anyway, let's show our appreciation and dump our things in it, and then we'll go over and pay respects to the chief.'

'Any chance of a tidy-up?' Gina asked, not fancying the idea of meeting anyone in her hot and sticky state, and glancing longingly at the smooth coolness of the river.

Perez followed her glance. 'I wouldn't advise it,' he told her quietly.

Disappointment shadowed her face. 'Oh?'

'Not unless you fancy being mauled by a catfish, or squeezed to death by an anaconda. It's up to you, of course.'

'No thanks.' Gina shuddered, turning away from the tempting water.

'Look out for chiggers, as well!'

'Chiggers?'

'Yes. Nice little chaps that burrow into your skin and produce their young. They'll fancy a nice fresh piece of white skin, I shouldn't wonder.' He spoke with a touch of amused condescension, but Gina ignored him – she was far too busy praying that her cans of insect repellent would hold out.

Out of the corner of her eye, she had seen Elena enter the

House of Strangers, no doubt to stake her claim to the most comfortable sleeping spot before the others arrived. Gina's blue eyes met Perez's and dismissed the mocking smile. 'Somehow,' she said slowly, walking past him and toward the house, 'these *chiggers*, as you call them, seem to remind me a little of someone.'

She moved on, Perez following behind. Sinon was still by the Toyota, watching the Indians unload their gear. As she walked, Gina suddenly felt a small tug at her skirt. She glanced down. An Indian boy of no more than four or five was looking up at her, a bright friendly smile on his brown face.

'Hello, who are you?' she asked in Portuguese. To her surprise, he answered in the same language.

'Luis.'

'Well, Luis, I'm very pleased to meet you.'

The House of Strangers had no door, and apart from four hammocks strung across the middle, there was nothing else in there. Nothing, that is, except for a huddle of brown blankets folded in a corner.

'Don't get too friendly with the natives,' Elena warned Gina sullenly, glancing at the boy. 'They're always after something, and if they think you're a soft touch, they'll never leave you alone.'

'I'll remember that,' replied Gina coldly.

Then Perez directed her to the 'wash-room': a partition of plaited leaves behind which stood a number of water-filled plastic buckets. He grinned as he saw her glance first at the buckets and then back at the hammocks. He chuckled as he said, 'That's right, we all wash and sleep together here. Don't worry, you'll be quite safe.'

Gina shrugged. 'I'm not worried.'

She tidied herself as best she could, wiping away the sticky grime with her still-damp sponge and combing her hair back from her face, holding it secure with a white towelling headband.

Later, she followed Elena outside again to where the two men were waiting – and little Luis.

'Who's your friend?' asked Perez, casting a wary eye at the boy.

'He says his name is Luis.'

The boy smiled up at her with his great brown eyes.

'Better not get too friendly.'

'Why not?'

'They train the children well.'

'Don't you like children?' She was pretty sure of the answer.

'Not much.'

He spoke rapidly to the boy in his dialect, and the child broke away, turning to run back toward the House of Strangers. But Gina called the boy back, and Perez smiled inwardly. He should have known she would like kids. How different the two girls were. He couldn't imagine Elena being interested in a child.

They walked together across the compound toward another house. One by one they entered, and even through the gloom, the sight made Gina gasp as the tall Indian chief rose to meet them.

'Treat him with respect,' hissed Perez.

Santana stepped forward to greet them. Circling his arm, he invited them to sit on the stools, cut from the solid wood of the forest, that were set before him in a semicircle. He made sure they were comfortable before returning to his own.

'*Corimagua!*' he said, his voice deep and his smile slow.

'*Corimagua,*' responded Perez, turning to Gina with the whispered translation. 'The chief says he is your friend.'

'I'm relieved to hear it,' she whispered back. She smiled nervously, nodding to Santana, '*Corimagua.*'

She hitched an arm around her knees, watching enthralled as the men began talking. Sinon seemed to be doing most of it, interrupted now and then by some terse remark from Perez.

Santana fascinated her. The chief was tall; very tall for an Indian. And his body was covered in tiny triangles of fibre, his skin blood red with the *ucuru* dye. His head was adorned with magnificent yellow plumes, falling down his back to the floor and trailing off into a bright rainbow of macaw feathers. She wondered if he would be too sensitive or proud to be photographed before they left. She hoped not, but knew that superstition ran deep among these primitive people.

The conversation ended some thirty minutes later, and when they went outside again, Gina began to play with the delighted Luis. Elena looked on, her face sullen, betraying her thoughts. The Matheson girl was too soft. Did she think Perez would be impressed by her fondness for children? If so, she was mistaken. Perez wanted only one thing from women, and she wanted to give it to him. She was quite sure that children played no part in the Perez scheme of things!

Later, back in the House of Strangers, Gina bathed herself with relief, not caring about the crudity of the buckets. She poured the water over her naked body, amused at the interest little Luis was showing in her block of soap. She didn't really feel embarrassed that he was watching. After all, he was used to seeing women naked. When she'd finished, he followed her.

It was a strange party that dined together that night. The sun had long set behind the western trees, yet it was barely any cooler. It was clear that Santana had laid on the welcome supper, although he himself did not join them. Mats were spread under open palm shelters behind the chief's house, and as they ate, a line of painted women stamped out a dance, chanting of the old Amazon and the lost people of the Xingu.

A large grey pot patterned with pictures of the forest's animals was set before them. Inside was a stew, and as she ate, Gina recognised the taste of fish. To accompany it were the inevitable pancakes of cassava flour, flavoured with a herb that Gina had never tasted before.

'How do you like it?' asked Perez.

'It's fine.'

'Better than the usual stuff they serve up,' Elena commented.

When the meal was over, Elena disappeared back into the House of Strangers. Perez and Sinon had gone off with Santana, leaving Gina sitting alone. Alone except for Luis.

A movement behind her made her turn. A girl was standing there; hardly more than a child, and with a baby at her breast. She called the little boy, who ran to her. Gina stood up, smiling. 'You have a fine son in Luis.'

The girl also understood Portuguese, and her smile widened. 'Yes,' she answered softly, turning and disappearing into the darkness of the commune.

Gina strolled toward the river, listening to the night sounds of the forest. Suddenly she felt the hard little brown hand of Luis creep into hers. She should be tired, but she wasn't. How could she sleep in this wonderful place?

'Lady! Lady!' Luis was suddenly tugging at her hand, leading her forward toward the river and a tall tree stump protruding from the inky water. 'Look, lady!'

Gina looked, and saw a great snake coiling its bulky length around the tree, poised to make its graceful entry into the water. Luis pulled her nearer and nearer, his brown face animated now and his small frame so strong that Gina could hardly hold him back. 'No! Luis! No!'

Her foot twisted painfully as she slipped further into the mud. She heard Luis' warning yell as she fell helplessly, the bank giving way easily under her, and for one terrifying moment she thought she would be sucked down. Then a strong hand was suddenly dragging her up again and into Perez's arms.

'What the hell are you playing at?' he growled. 'Didn't I tell you to keep away from the river?'

'I ... I ...'

'Another minute and you would have been in!'

' I'm sorry. ..'

'I want lady to see,' Luis' piping little voice shrilled. 'Look! Look!' He pointed to the half-submerged anaconda.

Perez turned grimly to the boy. 'Go to your mother, Luis.'

After a moment's hesitation, the child ran off toward the compound, leaving Gina to face Perez's scolding. He was still holding on to her arm.

'Don't do anything like that again,' he ordered, his voice tense.

Gina shook her head. 'I won't. I promise!' Suddenly, she knew she daren't look at him. It was very quiet now, the moon shining down like a spotlight and not a breeze stirring. As Perez moved his arm closer around her, she felt a spark inside at the pressure, which sent her blood throbbing in response. Suddenly they were just a man and a woman alone in this land of cruel beauty.

For God's sake! Perez told himself. *Don't be such a fool!* Yet he still held her, the silence stretching out between them. Then he jerked his hand away. His voice hard and flat, he said, 'Come on, let's get some sleep.'

They walked back to the commune, the tension broken. Gina still couldn't speak, aware of the shocked tingle in her stomach. Her mind was racing. Fear of the danger she'd been in and the memory of the warm, strong touch of his hands had so easily stripped away her reason or thought. She could no longer deny that she was attracted to him! Perhaps even more than that? But her stifled common sense was telling her, too, that this was merely an interlude in her life – wonderful and exciting, but an interlude all the same. She laughed lightly. 'You're certainly earning your money, looking after me.'

Perez glanced her way briefly, his eyes a quick blaze of black fire. 'I intend to.'

'Luis seemed to want to get in the river with the snake?'

'It's a game the village boys like playing. Mainly in their imagination. They slip onto the snake's back and ride him down the river. It's a calculated dare. But they don't get a real chance very often. Anacondas like to be private. This one probably had a full belly. Half asleep.'

'You're joking!'

'No, I'm not! Luis wanted to be like the bigger boys tonight – he wanted to ride that snake to impress *you*.' He flashed her another grim look. 'He wants you to admire him. Doesn't every male want to be admired? Even at five years old?'

They didn't speak again until they reached the House of Strangers. 'Goodnight, Perez, and ... and thank you,' said Gina. If it hadn't been for him, twice that day she could easily have been dead.

'No need for thanks,' he murmured. 'Just get a good night's sleep.'

'I will.'

She left him outside and went into the house. Undressing and swinging herself up into her hammock, she felt a movement below her. Looking down, she saw a pair of brown eyes. Luis hadn't been put off.

In the chief's house, Santana and Sinon sat together on the straw mat. 'Satisfied, Santana?' The Greek heaved up his huge bulk. 'You'll be rich after this trip!'

The silent Santana stared impassively. But Sinon knew that no-one had a greater desire for money than the Indian, and for that reason alone, he could depend entirely upon his loyalty.

The Greek smiled to himself. His expeditions with Perez were the best cover he could have. The police and the military were far too occupied with the cocaine trade to bother with the poaching of animal skins. Yet it was still dangerous. Selling pelts was lucrative, but as soon as he could fill his storehouse in Manaus, he would be happy – until the next trip. The money the Indian earned paid for guns, and helped him in his first-string trade too. Cocaine!

The two men shook hands, and Sinon left. As he went into the House of Strangers, he glanced at the sleeping Elena. *One day*, he thought, *I'll be rich enough even for you, my sweet. But will I want you then?*

He moved toward Gina, noticing that she was still awake, and saw the Indian brat sleeping on the floor beneath her, curled up like a puppy. 'What's the matter, Gina, can't you sleep in the jungle Hilton?'

Her blue eyes held his, cold and uninviting. 'I'm fine, Sinon.'

'I could help you.'

Gina turned away, and Sinon smiled. He'd bet the English girl was no different from other females. Perhaps, on the trip ahead, she'd change her mind about him.

When Sinon had gone to his hammock, Gina lay quietly in

hers. She looked across to where Perez lay sleeping on his back, the moonlight bathing his chest and shoulders. Gina was grateful for the dark, which allowed her to think about him privately. Whatever happened between them from now on, it was likely to be the greatest adventure she'd ever undertaken.

7

Gina stared up through the palm-leaves of the roof and into the dawn's light, wondering what the day would bring. The morning was already hot and still – not a breath of wind – and below her, coiling around the *maloca's* earth floor, was a haze of ground mist, pervading the wide hut and shrouding it with a distinct feeling of ghostliness.

Last night, before she had settled down to sleep finally, she had written a long letter to her father. She had told him of their journey so far; of what she had seen; of her companions. And later, reading it back, she had smiled a little, realising that most of it had been in praise of Perez; of his strength; of his knowledge of the Xingu. *Have I got it that bad?* she thought. She glanced now toward her companions. Perez was already up and his hammock empty. Sinon and Elena were still asleep.

In repose, the Greek girl's face was beautiful. She looked even more perfect now that the hard glitter of her dark eyes was veiled by her translucent lids. Her hair was black with russet undertones. She even lay like a sleeping cat, sleek and mysterious.

Then Gina almost jumped out of her skin. But it was only Luis. Next moment he was gone, his form a small grey shadow disappearing into the dawn's light. Gina shook her head and made her way to the buckets that were becoming second nature. Then ,when she was ready, she picked up her camera and went outside.

Perez stood in her way. 'Did you manage to sleep after all the excitement?' he asked.

'Like a log,' she lied.

'Good. More pictures?'

'I'd like to, if we have time?'

He glanced briefly at his watch. 'I'd intended to be off in an hour, but knowing those two ...' he nodded toward the *maloca*, '... it'll probably be some time before they're ready.'

Gina shrugged. 'In that case, I'll have time to take plenty.'

The village was already intent on its day's work. The Xingu's tributary was an important part of the trading network, and now, as Gina strolled away from Perez, she saw that the banks were already bobbing with the Indians' bark canoes, preparing for their fishing trips. Her camera clicked incessantly as she tried to capture the scene, and soon Perez strolled up to stand beside her as she worked.

'The men will be away for many days,' he told her. 'There will be no fish for the women until they come back.'

'What do they eat in the meantime?' Gina aimed her lens at the group of women in the makeshift field behind the commune, digging up the heavy roots of the manoic plants. 'Cassava?'

'That's right. They'll make *beju* cakes –j and pep them up with a few clam shells ...' He grinned, watching her face, '... Not to mention the odd howler monkey.'

Gina grimaced, and turned away as a roar sent her looking toward the river. The village boys were playing some kind of game, their smooth brown bodies thrashing about in and out of the water as they practised their warrior's chants. Some of the older youths were covered in white clay painted with black patterns, and their whooping voices reached screaming pitch as they ran and hopped, flapping their arms in the action of the birds.

'They learn early that even existence is tough; that life can be cruel. But here, playing like this, they learn too that life can be fun, sometimes,' Perez explained.

As though from nowhere, Gina felt Luis' hand come into

hers again. 'Come, lady. Come and watch.' A tiny bird was perched upon his shoulder.

'What a pretty little thing.'

'It's a kiskadee,' informed Perez, spotting Gina's interested look.

Gina stroked its blue and yellow breast. 'I've noticed most of the boys with one. Are they some kind of tribal thing?'

Perez laughed. 'These Xingu kids will make pets out of anything – except caiman; they're not so friendly.'

Luis was growing impatient and pulled again at her hand. 'See me, lady! Watch me!'

Gina glanced to where he was pointing; to the bank of dark shallows where they had seen the snake. 'Not again, thank you very much, Luis,' she grinned. 'I'll take your word for it that you can ride the anaconda.'

'Come! Come on!'

She looked back at Perez, hesitating. 'Shall I? You have to admit it would make a good picture.'

Perez shrugged. 'If you like. But watch where you're going.'

'I'll certainly do that!' Gina laughed, turning back to the Indian boy. 'Okay Luis, lead me to your friends.'

A delighted Luis led her toward the chanting boys as they played their war games. 'Wait here, lady.' He placed his finger under the tiny claws of the kiskadee and perched it on a branch. Then, with another of his bright, wide-gapped grins, he left her standing under a jatoba tree, safe from the river's edge, as he ran to join his fellows. From her vantage point, Gina clicked away with her camera. Soon, the dark, shiny back of the sleepy anaconda moved slowly along the bank toward Luis, who was poised and wary, waiting for the moment when it would either attack or slide off into the dark waters of the river.

Gina paused, holding her breath as Luis held his ground. The other boys gathered round, stamping the orange earth with excitement, knowing that this was Luis' first snake. Now the roles were reversed, as attacker became the attacked. Then, with amazing agility, Luis leapt across the back of the snake.

Silently, snake and rider slid into the river, while the boys on the bank, chanting Luis' success, followed them into the river's shallows. The triumphant Luis rode for about three metres before throwing himself off the writhing serpent and making his dash to the bank. He submerged momentarily, reappearing with a grin as he thrashed the water and waved his arms toward the bank.

'Look out, Luis!' Gina screamed. The anaconda had turned. 'Swim, Luis!'

She ran to meet him, while around her, the happy chanting had now ceased and the air was filled with the whistling sound of hand-made spears. Then Gina saw the lightning flash of silver that was boiling around Luis' thrashing feet. The young warriors rushed to pull him out.

'Catfish!' Perez ran past her and knelt beside Luis. Then his voice lashed the terrified Gina like a whip. 'Get Caninde! Tell him to radio the airstrip! Tell him what's happened and that we'll need a chopper! Now!'

Gina fled. Behind her came confused cries, but she was too shocked to care. Luis must be seriously hurt. He just *had* to survive!

When Perez carried Luis back to the commune a little while later, Santana was already waiting with the boy's mother.

'What shall we do?' Gina asked helplessly. 'How can we help him out here?'

'Let's pray Caninde got through and they'll have a chopper here soon. It'll be a rough ride, but it's his only chance. He's lost a lot of blood. Then my friend in Cachimbo will get a plane to take him down to Belem.' Perez cursed silently. To him, death was an old adversary. 'It's lucky we were here,' he muttered. 'He was losing too much blood.' All the time he was talking, Perez was applying the bandages they carried with them, while comforting the boy.

Then, raising him into a sitting position, Perez reached once more into the medical pouch, pulling the waterproof cover off a hypodermic needle with his teeth. He injected a morphine ampoule into the boy's arm, and when he had finished, the Indians carried Luis to the Toyota.

'That's all I can do for now,' he said to Gina. 'Getting him out of here is going to be rough! Let's hope the chopper gets here in time!'

Gina glanced across at the boy's young mother. She stood silently weeping. Soon Sinon and Elena appeared. Gina felt terrible, blaming herself for not stopping Luis going into the river. *Please, don't let him die!'* she prayed. He was so young.

'Will he be all right?' she asked, her voice wobbling.

'If our luck holds, the chopper'll be here soon.' Perez looked extremely worried. She had never seen him that way before. *So, things affect you after all,* she thought. *And you said you weren't keen on children. I saw your tenderness!* 'How long does it take to get here from the airstrip?'

'Fifteen minutes should do it. Fred will need to radio a helicopter if there isn't one there already.'

'Fred?'

'The guy who runs the strip.'

Gina glanced at Luis again. Blood was still oozing from the makeshift bandages. She stroked his shoulder with her finger, while Jeronimo bathed the boy's forehead with a cloth soaked in brackish water.

Perez reached out his hand to her. 'You've gone pale. There's some brandy in my flask.'

'No, thanks,' said Gina.

The Sikorsky helicopter pointed its nose straight for the clearing, and its rotors stilled as the man jumped out. 'There's a plane waiting at Cachimbo,' Fred Armstrong said, as he helped Perez with the boy. 'Sheila's aboard. She'll come with us as far as Cachimbo, and we've morphine if the kid needs more.'

Perez nodded brusquely as they lifted Luis onto the Sikorsky, giving the pilot a brief run-down on the treatment he'd had so far.

Armstrong was short and stocky, his face scored with wrinkles come from life in a punishing climate. Then Gina saw a woman's face appear momentarily at the porthole window.

Fred grinned. 'See? Sheila's more than organised. Everything's in hand.'

'Don't waste any time, Fred. The boy's in a bad way.'

'I can see that.' He glanced at Perez sharply. 'What's the matter, Perez? You've seen this sort of thing before. Are you losing your nerve?'

'Of course not! I just wish these kids would stop trying to prove themselves all the time.'

The man shrugged. 'You'll never stop them. But leave him to us now – we've got everything standing by.' He climbed back on board. 'Take care, you hear?'

Perez nodded and stood back as the rotors began to spin. 'I will.'

Suddenly Gina ran forward. 'Please! One second!' She thrust her hand deep into her pocket, bringing out the creased envelope that contained the letter to her father. 'If you get a chance, would you post this for me at Cachimbo?'

Fred reached out for the letter, glancing cursorily at the address. 'Sure, no problem. So, you know Colin Matheson?'

'He's my father.'

'Well, well. I heard he had a kid, but I didn't realise that the kid was a girl – and a beautiful one at that! But what the hell are you doing out here?'

Gina smiled. 'Communing with nature.'

'Well, keep close to Perez. No-one knows the forests better than he does – he's almost an Indian.'

'I will. And thanks for taking the letter.'

'No trouble, Miss Matheson, it's my pleasure. Besides, there's bound to be a company plane hanging around at Cachimbo. And if you get the chance, call in at the airstrip to see us. My wife would like that. It'll be a change for her to talk to someone like you instead of Perez's usual girlfriends.' A tiny throb of disappointment struck Gina. How many had he had?

The helicopter's rotors accelerated and it wheeled away, then circled and disappeared over the trees.

'Poor little devil,' remarked Perez. 'All we can do for him now is pray.' His face looked strained.

'What would have happened to Luis in the days before choppers?'

'He would have died! It's the law of the jungle! I suppose Fred's Sikorsky is one plus for civilisation.'

'I didn't know about the airstrip,' she said as they made their way back to the chief's house. 'And he knew Dad.'

Perez looked at her, hands thrust into his pockets and a frown on his face. 'Why shouldn't he?' he answered. 'Especially as his company are always sending people to spy out the land.'

'You hate our company, don't you?'

'Yes.'

She smiled slightly. 'Well, at least you don't mince your words.'

'They're destroying the forests,' replied Perez.

'I know, but others are destroying them, too.'

'Baxter-Weber are the worst.'

'In this area, perhaps,' Gina agreed softly. 'And for what good it does, I've told them what I think about it. I've spent hours trying to persuade Mark Baxter to change the company's policy.' She smiled up at Perez. 'You never know, perhaps some of it will get through that thick skull of his one day.'

'Probably when it's too late! And, knowing Baxter as I do, I doubt it. But I suppose trying to talk to him about it is better than doing nothing at all.'

She shot him a look. 'I've spoken to more people than Mark Baxter!'

He paused then, regarding her in a moment's thoughtful silence before he said, 'The forests mean a lot to you, don't they?'

Gina flopped down on a old dead stump and ran her hands through her hair. She sighed deeply. 'Yes, they do. And I'm not quite the damn useless butterfly you think I am. I don't want the Xingu to finish up like Rondonia.' It was one of the worst places for deforestation.

'It won't if I've anything to do with it. The loggers seem to be making a good living out of it. You've really done your homework.'

Gina thought she could hear a tiny bit of admiration in his praise. 'Yes, I have. And publishing these pictures of the Xingu might add more pressure to the cause.' She started to walk away, and Perez got up to follow. 'At least I'm doing something! I'm not sitting at home on my backside and just talking about it!'

He slipped an arm lightly around her shoulder, an amused smile playing around his mouth. 'I wonder if the authorities realise just what they're taking on?' With his arm about her, she knew she had found both comfort and protection.

They stopped outside the chief's house. 'How did you come to know Fred Armstrong?'

'We used to work for Pan Am,' he answered casually. 'We bumped into each other a few times when I did a stint with the same airline – that's how I came to be flying around Rondonia.'

'And Sheila?'

'His wife. She used to be a nurse. When Fred gave up his Pan Am job, the two of them started their own business and bought a lump of land here off Highway 080. Fred's a bit of an opportunist. He could see the profits to be made in moving equipment and people around quickly, and they've done quite well. He's helped me out a couple of times, too.' He turned away then, leaving her standing alone as he went into the chief's house.

Up in the helicopter, Sheila Armstrong pulled the sheet further around the sleeping Luis. 'Who was that girl with Perez?"

'Colin Matheson's daughter.'

'It's the first time I've known Perez to show any interest in a European.'

'Do you think I didn't notice? We men aren't as unobservant in matters of the heart as you women think. We can see just as well as any woman when another guy has a girl on his mind.'

'Perez needs a good woman. Especially after Dorita.'

'Don't start matchmaking! What Perez feels for young Miss Matheson is nothing to do with us.'

Sheila Armstrong laughed softly, patting her husband's hand. 'I know, but it would be nice to see him settled. Do you think he's interested in the girl more than he should be?'

He shrugged. 'Who knows? No doubt he'll tell us in his own good time.'

'I hope so. I like Perez, and he deserves a break.'

'You're a woman, Sheila – and what woman wouldn't like a guy like Perez, eh?'

Sheila ruffled her husband's wiry grey hair. 'He's almost as good-looking as you, Fred.'

Fred chuckled. 'No-one is as good looking as me!'

The helicopter began its descent, and as Sheila went back to her charge, she wondered again about Perez and Gina Matheson. They had looked so good together.

She sighed, stroking the little boy's black hair away from his face. You could never tell with Perez. He was a law all to himself!

'I need to get some air, before I settle down for the night,' said Gina.

'Don't go near the river, then,' ordered Perez.

'I think you know I won't,' she answered, going outside.

Perez went to the wash-house and poured a bucket of water over himself. 'Damned heat!' he cursed. 'I'll never get used to it!'

Sinon was lying alone in his hammock. 'I didn't think it mattered to you.'

'It matters.'

'You could always go back.'

'Back to where? To Rio? Brasilia? Not me!'

'What about England?'

Perez laughed roughly. 'Perhaps, one day.'

'You'll die here. You'll never leave this godforsaken place.'

Perez laughed again, swinging himself up into his hammock. 'You're probably right.' He looked at his watch again. 'The accident to the boy's delayed us at least a day.' He turned onto his side, pulling over the mosquito net. 'Anyway, we'll make up for it – we'll have to, time's running out – I've only been paid for a month.'

'Where's Elena?'

'Who knows? Mixing with the natives?'

The men glanced at each other. Then Sinon turned over, hoping Perez wouldn't be too much trouble, as he had to get into the Xingu – and fast. Perez didn't have to know about the illegal pelts. That was Sinon's private business – Sinon's and Santana's. Why come all this way just because his friendship with the chief guaranteed an unmolested trip? Why not make a nice little bit on the side as well? He turned restlessly. *Where the hell is Elena?*, he thought.

8

'Okay! Okay! Come on, everybody! Time to get up!'

Gina stirred, feeling the sway of her hammock as a hand pushed against it. She blinked open her eyes. 'What time is it?'

'Sunrise – time to get moving.' She eased herself up as Perez pushed against the sleeping Greek. 'Come on, Sinon, rouse yourself!'

Yawning and pulling down the T-shirt that served as a nightdress, Gina swung herself out of the hammock. Outside, she could hear the sound of rain. It seemed always to be raining in this river-land. It was as if the whole vast area of the Xingu was dominated by two significant features – forest and water!

Resigning herself to another soaking day, she passed Elena's hammock to go to the wash-room and cast a bleary glance at the waking girl. Suddenly, she had a feeling of foreboding. Elena looked pale and worn out. She lay on her back, her gaze empty as she stared up at the straw roof.

'Are you all right?' Gina asked, pausing by the hammock.

'Fine.' Elena sat up, her voice little more than a croak in her throat. 'I'm still tired, that's all. Leave me alone.'

Gina shrugged, wondering what has kept Elena out so late. She was used to the Greek girl's rudeness by now. And moments later she was stripping off her T-shirt and pouring the tepid water over her sluggish frame.

Drying herself, Gina pushed aside the plaited grass screen and dressed. One of the Indian women had already brought in the morning's pancakes of cassava flour, and Gina made short work of appeasing her jungle-jaded palate. Fifteen minutes later, when she went outside the *maloca*, she was glad to see that the rain had stopped and that Perez and the Indians were almost ready for the trip.

Perez turned as she approached, his eyes flicking over her brief khaki shorts. 'Those are no good.' The admiration in his eyes set off a thrill inside her.

'What do you mean?'

'The leeches will have a field day. Wear something that will cover your legs.'

Gina glared at him for a moment. Although she was offended, she knew he was being sensible, and she went back inside to change into her jeans. Elena was still in her hammock, making no attempt to get dressed. Gina thrust her legs into a pair of thick denims, and asked, 'Are you getting up or not? We're all ready, apart from you.'

'I'm not coming.'

Gina swung round. 'What?'

'I said, I'm not coming. I'm ill. I have a fever.'

Gina looked at her anxiously. The girl certainly looked pale. Her face was ashen, and dark rings were shadowing her eyes. 'Does Perez know?'

There was a movement behind her, and Gina turned abruptly at the sound of Perez's deep voice. 'Yes. I know. And if you're worried about the cost, I'll see that your father gets a discount. I've already checked Elena out, and it's nothing serious – just a slight touch of jungle belly. But if we were to take her like this, it would hold us up. She's better staying here until we get back.' The girl was smiling now, weakly perhaps, but smiling nonetheless.

'Ought we to radio Fred again?' asked Gina. 'Couldn't he pick her up in the chopper?'

'No. She's not that ill.' Elena made a face.

'But wouldn't she be better off at the airstrip and away from here?'

Elena stared at Gina. 'I've already had this out with Perez.

It's better that I stay here.' Evidently she didn't intend to explain, as she turned her back on them.

As she and Perez walked out of earshot, Gina was wondering what to do about it. She wanted to argue. After all, her father had put a lot of money into this trip. But, privately, she knew that she could do nothing. She didn't want to push the girl if she really preferred to stay. Yet a gut feeling was telling her that Elena's sudden illness was deceptive. The Greek girl was pale – that was true enough – but she didn't seem as ill as she was making out. Gina wondered why Elena was going to such lengths to stay behind. There had to be a reason. Surely the girl, who Gina knew was jealous, wouldn't relish the thought of herself and Perez being alone together in the jungle! Gina shrugged. Whatever the reasons were, there wasn't a damn thing she could do about it! She snapped her wilting travelling bag shut. 'What about Sinon? Is he still coming with us? Or is he too ill to finish the trip, too?'

Perez inclined his head. 'You bet your life he's coming! Even if he were dead on his feet, I'd drag him along. He's too useful to leave behind. Without him, we could really run into trouble.'

'What kind of trouble?'

'With the other Indian tribes around the Xingu – especially the Tskikao!'

'Has he such influence?'

Perez glanced quickly at Elena, then back at Gina again, commenting quietly, 'I'm afraid he has. Sinon is necessary.' His face was expressionless. 'I'm not trying to alarm you, but I think you ought to know of the dangers we could face for the next few days. The fact that we're strangers in their land is a risk in itself – we're a big threat. But, contrary to popular belief, the Indian's greatest enemy is another Indian – always has been – and they depend on Sinon.

'An Indian can't stroll down to the supermarket for a couple of pounds of potatoes. His food comes from the forest and the river. Tribes face fierce competition from each other. They think nothing of killing anything that threatens their means of survival – especially other Indians.'

Gina sighed. 'But how can Sinon help?'

'He oils the wheels. They help him in his trade, and he pays them well. They need him and his money!' Perez frowned and turned away. 'I hope I've made myself clear.'

'Perfectly. What does Sinon do?'

'He has a deal with Santana.'

'What kind of deal?'

'That's strictly between the two of them. But I'm pretty sure the chief uses Sinon's money for arms.'

'Arms?' Gina was shocked.

He sighed a little impatiently. 'Yes, arms. Guns. Those things that go bang-bang.'

She felt angry suddenly. He was treating her like a child. And she wanted him to see her as a woman! She felt her cheeks go red. 'To kill other Indians?'

Perez shrugged. 'That happens frequently.'

'It's crazy.'

'It takes all sorts out here!'

'It's brutal and senseless.'

'Brutal, yes! Senseless, no! To an Indian, it makes a lot of sense. It helps keep their numbers down.'

Gina gritted her teeth. 'Doesn't disease keep them down enough without us selling them guns?'

'Guns are what they want.'

'So that they can kill each other more quickly?'

Perez forced a faint smile. 'This is not an ideal world.'

'And we're not helping,' Gina snapped back.

Ignoring her bleak expression, Perez went on quietly, 'Having Sinon along is merely a precaution. I don't like it any more than you do. But don't forget, I'm being paid to look after you. You're my responsibility.'

'You don't have to keep reminding me. You're making me feel like I'm a burden.'

He gave a deep sigh, his face hardening. 'You don't know how much of a burden, Miss Matheson,' he finished softly.

Perez strode out into the commune, leaving Gina to get her things together. He had little enthusiasm for Sinon's dirty business. He hadn't enjoyed giving Gina the impression that he condoned Sinon's trade, but there was damn all he could do about it now!

He reached the waiting Indians, his face grim. She had no room to talk! She knew what Baxter-Weber were doing to the Indians as well! Hell, what was the matter with him? It was as though he wanted the girl's approval!

Gina heard Elena's soft laugh behind her, and she turned quickly to face her. 'What's so funny?'

The girl shrugged. 'You are, little English mouse. This expedition is no longer about the forest, is it?'

'What are you talking about?'

The girl's dark eyes narrowed. 'You know damn well why. It's all about Perez now, isn't it?'

Sinon spoke abruptly to the bearers as they shouldered their supplies. Gina waited, watching as Chief Santana emerged from his house and walked over to Sinon. The two men were in deep conversation for several minutes, their voices low, and then the chief nodded conspiratorially before returning to his house. And as the little group finally made their way out of the commune, Gina saw the shadowed form of Elena watching every movement. The Greek girl's eyes remained fixed on them until they had moved out of sight to take the forest trail that would lead them to the tributary.

Sinon followed Gina's gaze. 'Don't worry about Elena,' he murmured softly in her ear. 'I know she has her reasons for staying behind. And you will be safe with me.'

'Will I, Sinon?' Gina countered coldly. 'I wonder!'

Sinon laughed smoothly. 'Yes, my little one. You will need me before this trip is out, I think.' Then he was off to join Perez, leaving Gina with a nasty taste in her mouth. The man was a slime ball!

Soon they were moving in single file through one of the

wildest places on planet Earth; on through the twilit interior of the forest, where few flowers grew in the sun-starved soil. Nothing intruded in this place. Looking up into the dense canopy of treetops, through the scant sombre light, Gina saw at last the aerial garden of orchids and fragrant passion flowers, their perfume wafting down through the humid air below.

For Gina, the jungle suddenly took on a great beauty. Her camera's flash captured forever the leaf mosaics, the crinum lilies, and the glory of the poisonous nightshade. And, here and there, through the watery clearings, the delicate pink and purple hues of the still water hyacinths.

It took over three hours to reach the tributary, and as they climbed onto the narrow rafts that were waiting there, Perez handed Gina the map. 'Here, take this, I don't need it now.'

She glanced down at it. 'Whereabouts are we?'

'We're here.' He stabbed a finger at the point. 'From here on, I'm relying on my sixth sense.' He paused, grinning at Gina's doubtful glance. 'It's never let me down before.'

'There's a first time for everything.'

He checked his watch, adding reassuringly, 'Don't worry. If I can't make it, the Indians can. They know this area.'

They pushed their way along the tributary. To Gina's city-bred brain, it seemed impossible that so much water should be trapped in this basin; almost as much as the whole of the water in the world. But, as she looked around, she marvelled at the wonder of it all. On either side of her, great walls of vegetation sprang up, silent and forbidding. Like tiny dragonflies on the shimmering water, the three rafts pushed on, Gina, Perez and Caninde in the leading one and Sinon, Jeronimo and the other Indian porters ensconced in the other two.

Perez lifted his eyes and looked at Gina. There was a grace in the way she sat, one hand tightly holding her camera and the other coiled loosely around her denimed knee. He liked the eager sparkle in her eyes and the forward thrust of her breasts beneath the wine-coloured shirt. Her cheeks were flushed, and her shining blonde hair tumbled down her back, escaping its restraint of the cotton bandeau.

He turned away, glad that she had not noticed or felt his aching, hungry eyes upon her. And when she next looked back at him, his eyes were downcast as he frowned in thought. 'We'll strike camp in another hour,' he informed her. 'You'll have your first real taste of the forest by night.'

'I can't wait.'

Perez scowled. 'I'll bet. Especially as you'll have only me for company for most of it.'

Gina looked at him sharply, trying to ignore the sensuality of his mouth. 'What do you mean? Where will the others be?'

He answered her quietly. 'Brace yourself. Apart from Caninde and Jeronimo, the rest of our little party will be busy tonight. Sinon has his business to attend to.'

'Business?'

'This is ocelot country,' he explained grimly. 'And Sinon is partial to a bit of ocelot.'

Gina sucked in her breath. 'How does he get away with it? Surely the authorities ...' She broke off.

'It's a big place to police.'

'It's immoral!'

Perez held her angry gaze. 'I know.'

'Aren't you going to do anything about it?'

Her reproachful eyes hurt him. If only he could tell her how he felt. But he was only her guide. 'Are you?'

'I wish I could. But I'll report him when I get back.'

'Will you?' He was looking at her steadily, but there was no mockery in the gaze.

Gina turned away, looking out at the dense green forest around her, trying to control her feelings. Moments later, she turned back to Perez, asking, 'Does he hunt them himself?'

Perez laughed grimly. 'Not he! All he does is pick them up and pay Santana. The pelts are shipped down the tributary until they reach the river. Then they're loaded onto some stinking freighter.'

A moment later, the grey sky cracked with lightning. 'Here it comes,' Perez said. 'I was hoping to be off the river before the storm broke.'

Gina glanced up at the threatening sky. They had reached a sluggish part of the water, stagnant and almost like a large pond. It was littered with the debris of the forest – leaves, twigs, petals and insects – and reflecting the overhanging trees like a dull mirror. The rain came down in a sudden torrent, drenching them in seconds, and Gina shivered as she felt the cool, heavy drops soak through her inadequate shirt. Yet it was somehow thrilling! It was as though she was suddenly a part of the elements; a primitive fusion of nature!

Perez and Caninde swung themselves into the water, pushing the raft to the bank. Perez yelled to the other Indians, who did the same, and Gina reached out to pull at the undergrowth, steering them in. Then they moved inland for about half a mile to make camp for the night. By nightfall, after the storm had passed, Perez had settled for a steep bank of bare earth, broken only by a few fallen trees. Later, they dined on Caninde's special stew, boiled up on a primus stove.

Perez sat down beside Gina. 'How did you like the soup?'

Gina pulled a small face. 'I've had better.'

Perez grinned. 'Caninde's famous for that particular brew.'

'Why?'

'It gives you wonderful dreams if you eat enough of it.'

She turned to look at him, staring, her large eyes wide. 'Do you mean it's spiked?'

He laughed softly. 'A little. It helps to recover a man's energy mentally as well as physically. The Indians use the stuff all the time.'

'What the hell is it?'

'*Banisteriopsis* – they take it from a vine. The Indians believe that the images it produces are the source of the beginning of the world.'

She shook her head, thankful that the taste had been so sour that she'd taken only a little of it. 'You might have warned me.'

Perez grinned. 'It does no harm. Besides, I noticed you had only half a bowl.'

She looked toward Sinon, wondering what he was telling the

four Indians who stood around him. 'Do you think he'll be off soon?'

Perez nodded grimly. 'Yes, pretty soon. His payroll is on the back of the Indian next to him.'

Gina looked again, taking in the heavy leather bag on the porter's back. 'Is it money?'

'Partly. Whatever else, I've never found out for sure. But you'll find that Sinon never lets it out of his sight. When they come back, it'll be full of pelts.'

Sinon glanced across at them, as though he'd overheard. Gina made a silent vow. When she got back to Belem, she would make sure the authorities knew about him, and everything else connected with his filthy trade.

Sinon dismissed the Indians and strolled over to them. 'Has Perez told you I have a little business to attend to?'

'Yes, he has, Sinon, and it stinks.'

He laughed softly. 'But it pays well.'

She turned away, sickened. 'It's a hell of a way to make a living!'

Sinon leaned forward. 'So we don't see eye to eye, little one.' Gina jerked her head away as he went on, his tone hardening perceptively, 'And has Perez also told you what a useful and powerful companion I can be in this wilderness?'

'He's told me you are useful.'

He smiled. 'Oh, I am. And I shall be back before sunrise.'

The Greek turned away, calling to the Indians, and soon they were gone, swallowed up by the darkness.

Gina turned to Perez, flashing him a bright, jokey smile. 'Well, shall *we* make a night of it as well.'

A sapling flared in the fire, crackling and sparking. 'Yes,' he answered, his deep voice uncertain. He stood up, wiping his hands against his trouser leg. 'What would you like to do?'

Gina laughed. 'Do you mean I have a choice?'

He shrugged and grinned. 'Not much of one, but we could go for a walk if you like.'

'Where on earth to?'

'Along the river. Seeing as you're paying, you might as well see as much as you can.'

She stood up. 'Okay, lead on.'

'I'll carry that.' Perez slung her camera across his shoulder and took her arm. 'Stay close.'

The moon was directly overhead as they started to walk. It seemed to Gina, as she looked up at it, that it was playing some kind of desperate game. They walked in silence, almost as though they were the last two people on Earth and were afraid to break the stillness.

'Listen! Hear that?' Perez stopped abruptly, and Gina strained to hear the rustling sound.

'What is it?'

'I think it's a swamp deer. They usually come down to the river at night to feed on the reeds.'

They waited, but the creature remained elusive. After a while, they walked on, skirting the shore where the reptiles waited, dull shapes in the moon's light. Night birds were all around, hidden from sight in the high branches of the trees, and here and there Gina swore she could see the glow of eyes as they shone in the light of Perez's torch.

They stopped in a clearing not far from the camp. Here, the drift of their fire caught their nostrils, and Gina could still see the lights of the camp's sole source of illumination, the Tilley lamp. Perez turned his head abruptly, suddenly tense and aware of danger, his fingers tightening around the shaft of his rifle. 'Look! There!'

Gina peered into the wall of darkness, hardly daring to breathe. It was her first sight of a puma; and although Perez was ready, he didn't need to shoot.

The creature's glowing eyes held theirs. It held itself very still, more interested in the swamp deer than the two of them. Then, after those few, tense moments, it loped away toward the river, its velvet ears tight against its head as it went in search of its supper.

Gina exhaled her relief, the tension easing as she looked up at Perez. 'Beautiful!' she murmured. 'And I didn't get one picture!'

'Come on.' Perez took her arm, his knuckles brushing against the side of her breast as he did so. He walked on, conscious of the girl by his side and of her figure that seemed constantly to arouse him. He cursed silently, checking the impulse to take her into his arms. He was not sure how she would react.

When they returned to the camp, the tents had been pitched ready for the night, and the two Indians were fast asleep, dead to the world on their bowls full of spiked stew. And, by the look of their drugged expressions, they were already deeply communing with the source of life.

'Perhaps I should have had an extra helping,' Gina commented, stepping gingerly over them as she reached for her sleeping bag. 'I'd give anything to lie still like that for the next few hours.' She straightened up, her sweat-stained shirt moulded against her breasts, and wiped a hand across her forehead. 'Have we anything to drink?'

'There's some beer.' Perez moved away to get it. Instinctively, he was more than sure she would respond if he tried something; but, for the first time in his life, he didn't know how to handle it. When he came back with the beer, he sat down beside her, flipping open the cans and handing her one. He smiled. 'I thought you would have been asleep by now.'

Gina laughed softly, sipping the beer slowly, then balancing the can against a rock. 'I don't feel I'll ever sleep again.'

'Don't you?' They smiled at each other, and subconsciously he slid his arm around her. As she turned to look at him, her face half-surprise, half-expectant, he mouthed his apologies. A difficult position had now become impossible as he drew her face gently to his. Then, suddenly, she was in his arms. They kissed wildly, crazily, as if there was no time left before this wilderness faded away and the night was only a dream. For long, stunned minutes she buried herself in Perez's arms, not speaking. They held each other close, their silence saying more than a million words. Minutes later, they drew back, and Gina felt suddenly shy. A belated feeling of self-consciousness started on its ridiculous way, sweeping over her and making her feel like a love-sick adolescent.

'What now?' Perez whispered.

She shook her head. 'I ... I don't know ... '

'I didn't mean for this to happen,' he murmured.

'Neither did I.' She gave him a small smile, adding softly, 'But I'm glad it has.'

'So am I.'

Gently, Perez pushed her down. His hand, as though of its own volition, reached for the buttons of her shirt and slipped it from around her shoulders. He lowered his head to kiss her upturned face, and she didn't try to stop him. She made no move as his hand slid along her narrow waist, then upwards, pausing only to cup around her breast. The nipple hardened against his thumb, and he noticed for the first time the tiny beads of sweat glistening along her brow. He kissed them away, laughing softly and fumbling with the waistband of her thick jeans. 'Whoever suggested women should wear trousers ought to be shot.'

Gina grinned, unhooking the denims and shrugging them down to kick them away. 'You did, remember? But they're not really a problem.'

He paused above her, a hand stroking through the pale blonde hair that was falling about her shoulders. 'Are you sure about this, Gina? And I'll be careful. You'll be okay.'

He had his answer. Her arms came around his neck, pulling him closer down toward her.

The silence of that hot night was broken only by the whispering trees around them and the murmur of the river breaking gently against the banks below. They made love on the blanket that was spread on the ground, and later, when it was over, they lay wrapped in each other's arms, looking up at the stars. Gina turned on her side, her fingertips stroking along the side of Perez's cheek. His lips kissed them lightly, and they smiled at each other.

She moved her arms, circling them around his waist and pressing her face against his chest, breathing in deeply as the hard muscle of his arm came around her. She was safe with

Perez. As long as she was with him, nothing – and no-one – could touch her. They lay together like that for a long time, until Perez eased away his arm to prop his head on his elbow. He kissed Gina again. She was fast asleep now, her face flushed and beautiful from their lovemaking.

Perez lifted her into his arms, carrying her sleeping form into his tent. He laid her gently under the cover of the sleeping bag and placed the mosquito net over her face. When he was satisfied that she was safe from any predatory night intruder, after kissing her forehead, he climbed into his own bag and settled down to sleep.

Perez was up early, making coffee long before the Indians awoke. And after he'd brought it to Gina, he stroked her hair from her face. 'Okay?'

Gina smiled at him and sipped the near-cold coffee. 'Do you have any idea how good you've made me feel?' She had accepted him now. Any pangs of regret could come later, but she wouldn't forget their night together. He'd made her feel more than she'd ever dreamed.

He smiled, nodding comfortably in answer. 'I feel pretty good myself.'

She finished the coffee, not minding the taste, her mind straying to her life in Belem. She didn't want that kind of life anymore. She felt instinctively that her future would be inevitably meshed with Perez', and she wanted nothing to ever change that.

'You're looking serious,' he said. 'No regrets, I hope.'

She looked up, smiling. 'No. I was just thinking, that's all.'

'What about?

Gina looked at him again, her face pensive. 'I take this kind of thing seriously. I think you ought to know.'

He returned her gaze gravely. 'So do I! And I want you to know something too ...' He paused, searching for the right words and his eyes hardening a little, '... I want you, Gina. I want you here. By my side.'

His words washed over her like a caress. She smiled and answered softly, 'Okay.' Then she chuckled, adding teasingly. 'You'd better, after last night!'

As they joked together, the Indians awoke and prepared the morning's food. Within minutes, the clearing was alive with noise and activity.

And, as they sat together eating their fish, Gina's heart sank. Her paradise suddenly shattered as she saw the fat form of Sinon appear through the trees, the Indians following behind him, laden with the sacks of pelts. The Greek seemed in high spirits. He grinned at the two of them as he sat down beside them. 'Did you two enjoy yourselves while I was away?'

Perez stood up, his face grim. 'I take it your business was a success, Sinon.'

Gina glanced from one man to the other, comparing the soft, flabby body of the Greek with the lean and beautiful Perez.

'Complete success,' replied Sinon, his fat features still creased into what passed as a smile. 'But I'm tired now. Dealing with those savages is hard work. I'm getting my head down for a while.'

Apart from Caninde and Jeronimo, only one sole Indian remained in the clearing. He stood impassively by a tethered mule, and for some strange reason, as she caught the Indian's eye, Gina shivered. There was a threat in the man's silent presence, and it frightened her.

She looked round quickly for Perez. He was far away, over on the other side of the clearing, discussing the day's expedition with Caninde. Without him, Gina felt naked and afraid, wishing for one moment that she was far away from the unseen menace of the forest. But then she remembered what had happened between her and Perez and began to cheer up.

9

Sinon slept for most of the day, but woke just as the moon was rising again. He lay under his net for a while, too lazy to move, and lit a cigar. There were only two things on his mind at that moment: business and the girl in the neighbouring tent.

Finally the Greek threw back the flap and stepped into the dark. His business had been profitable and he was rested and alert. He felt so good, in fact, he could have done with a woman right then. Now both his mind and his eyes swivelled and fixed on Gina's tent. Perhaps he might be lucky?

When Perez and the girl had come back earlier, a plan had begun to form in Sinon's mind. He smiled to himself. He knew where they'd been. What they'd been doing! She'd said she wanted pictures for her book, and Perez had taken her to where there were butterflies and blossoms and all the pretty things. But what else had happened?

He had seen the look on their faces when he and Santana's Indians had come back in the morning. But he had to be careful. And she had to know that Perez wasn't the only man around. Sinon could give her a lot. And he knew what women were like. They smelled money a mile away. And he had it! Maybe she liked the taste of it too? It could buy her a good life anywhere in the world, and whatever she thought of him and his trade, the Greek was sure he could offer Gina Matheson enough dollars to make her forget her threats.

As for Perez, Sinon knew he wouldn't dare to go upriver

again without Sinon. He lit a cheroot, his mind drifting to the Indian girl he'd had the night before, who was more like a silent, proud animal than a woman. She'd been his reward from Santana.

Under normal circumstances he would have been satisfied, but Gina was different. He had never had sex with an English girl. He imagined that might be a challenge. What was she like really? He'd bet a million dollars her aloof attitude was just a front. Yes, she would do right now! It was more than pleasure just thinking about it. She was getting under his skin, and he wanted her! Just how far had she gone with Perez? He had seen the starry-eyed look on the girl's face whenever they were together. And as for Perez, never had Sinon seen him act toward anyone the way he was acting toward Gina Matheson. Not even Dorita. He inhaled deeply. Perhaps they were lovers already? It wouldn't surprise him. He took a swig of his brandy. He could wait.

'Gina, are you asleep?' She looked up. 'Gina?' She looked up and realised it was Sinon!

'What do you want? I'm tired!' she snapped.

'I think we should talk. There's something you ought to know ...'

'What?' Her tone was wary.

'It's about Perez.'

'Can't it wait until tomorrow?'

'It can. But it's more convenient now.'

Gina sighed deeply, hauling herself out of the sleeping bag and throwing on a robe. 'You'd better come in then, but make it quick.'

Sinon stepped through the tent flap, his eyes rolling over Gina and particularly the soft, tempting skin that beckoned through the thin cotton of her robe. Her neck and arms were brown from the sun but the rest of her was creamy-white; soft, warm and female. He felt his heart rate increase, as if he'd run a mile.

'You'll thank me for it,' he murmured.

'I doubt it,' she said, 'but get it off your chest anyway.'

He moved closer, and Gina backed away. He added, 'Perez is my friend, but all the same, there are things about him you ought to know.'

'Your *friend?*'

'Yes, my friend. He's a good guide. But there are some things that are not so good about him.'

'And is this is how you treat a friend? Talking about him behind his back?'

He grinned, his eyes narrowing, 'Perhaps I should say business acquaintance ,then? Shall we settle for that?'

'Before you go on, I think I should warn you that Perez is *my* friend! And I'm particularly loyal to the people I care about!'

'Perhaps he's not such a good friend as you imagine.'

'Stop waffling and get on with it, Sinon.'

'I've known Perez for a long time, and can tell when he's interested in a woman.' Gina remained silent, her face expressionless, as the Greek continued, 'I like you, my little one. I don't want to see you hurt.'

'Who'd want to hurt me?'

'Perez is not interested in you, except for one thing only. Can't you see what he's doing? You are here alone with him, and he's a man who ...'

Impatiently she turned away. 'Get out of here, Sinon!'

He raised a placating hand. 'No, hear me out. Perez is playing with you. The only girls Perez likes are Indians, but in the Xingu they're not easy to find, so it's quite convenient that you're on hand.'

'I've told you to get out of here! I don't want to hear any more!'

'But you should. I'm just being honest.' He reached out and fingered her robe. 'Surely you don't want to play second fiddle to an Indian girl, when I could give you so much?'

Gina's throat was suddenly bone dry. She stepped back, putting distance between herself and the offensive Greek. He wasn't smiling now. He was showing no emotion at all, yet the lust was oozing from him like filthy water.

'What about Elena? She isn't Indian!' Too late the words came out, and Gina couldn't take them back.

His voice was silky no longer. He stared and hissed, 'What do you know of Elena?'

She turned away slightly. ' I don't know anything about Elena. I don't know why I said that. You made me angry, that's all ...' She broke off.

He straightened up. 'It's a good thing you don't know anything about her. But you ought to know about Perez. I'm just warning you, that's all. Perez is lonely, little one. He has no woman now, and *you* are available.'

'Go away, Sinon.'

'Don't be angry,' the Greek said softly. 'Perez is handsome, yes? What girl could resist him? And you are here! I think I can already guess what has taken place between you both!'

Gina felt nauseated. How could she allow Sinon to go on like this? Only a few short hours ago, she and Perez had made the most wonderful love.

'Perez can sometimes be very careless,' he added.

'Careless?'

The dark eyes glittered as he looked down. 'Yes, Gina, careless. Allow me to tell you a little story. Once upon a time, there was a lovely young girl, and her name was Dorita ...'

That was enough for Gina! She leapt up, her eyes wide with hot, uncontrollable temper. 'Will you get the hell out of here, Sinon! I don't want to hear your fairy stories! Not now! Not ever!'

Sinon smiled. He had touched a nerve. And at last he had cracked the composure. 'I want you to know that you have Sinon to protect you.'

She laughed scornfully. '*You!*'

'Yes.' He was moving even closer. 'Be sensible, Gina. I'm powerful and wealthy. I could give you everything. Perez can give you nothing. Let Sinon show you what he can give you.'

Nervously, she looked round, searching for a way of escape. Should she scream and wake the camp? 'Leave me alone!'

'Now, let's be sensible,' he persisted. 'Please let us get to know each other better.' His scent was nauseous. All at once, Gina was very scared. She was about to scream, when his hand clamped over her mouth, and next moment he was pushing her down. It was her worst nightmare coming true, and she couldn't even shout for help!

Gina was no match for the Greek, however much she writhed and twisted against him. She had thought he was flabby, but he was also very powerful. Then, to her horror, he brought out a knife, which he held near to her nose. 'Such a pity I had to persuade you, Gina!' She struggled madly. 'It will be easier for us both if you don't fight me, little one.'

Her throat was full of silent curses. Her neck was aching and her body bruised to pieces. *Where the hell was Perez now she needed him? Oh, why didn't someone come?*

'That's better,' he said. With his free hand, he tore at her robe in a frenzy. Fear pumped her adrenaline, and Gina tried once more to fight back. He grinned at her futile struggles, his thick, coarse voice turning her blood to ice. The man was like a jackal ...

Every prayer she uttered then must have been answered. *'Gina!'*

Dazed, she saw the glint of Sinon's knife. 'Look out, Perez!'

With the strength of a big cat, Perez lunged at Sinon, who crashed back, winded. Perez kicked the knife away, picked up the camp stool and hurled it into Sinon's face. The two men stared at each other.

In that moment of safety and relief, Gina fled outside and retched, then lay on her back, staring blankly at the pure, clean treetops above her and at the little golden light of the lamp. She closed her eyes. The pain and the ache began to fade, as if she was passing out. The forest seemed to close in around her, protecting and loving her. Gina's head swam as she drifted in and out of consciousness.

The she felt rain on her face; not a sudden deluge that left her in wet misery, but a cool and cleansing shower that forced Sinon's smell away from her body. She lay, just letting the pure drops fall over and around her, washing her clean. Then she rolled on her side again and began to cry and rock hysterically.

'Here, drink this.' Perez lifted her chin, holding a flask to her bruised mouth. Gina shook her head. 'Drink it, Gina! It's only brandy.' He held it against her lips, forcing her to swallow. Then, gently, he lifted her body, as though she were a doll, and carried her to his tent. She clung to him, shaking all over. 'Don't be afraid. He'll give you no more trouble.' Perez unzipped his sleeping bag and motioned she get in. With his help, she obeyed. Then she lay in silence, eyes tightly closed ...

Perez looked down at her, his mouth tightening as he thought of Sinon. If only he hadn't been outside the clearing! But thank God he'd come back in time. He saw the bruises on her arms and her broken fingernails where she clutched the sleeping bag around her, just like a frightened child. He had never felt more at a loss. He'd been paid to protect her. And he'd failed in every way.

When morning came, Gina woke aching and stiff. As she remembered what had happened, she felt almost too sick to face another day. There was no sign of Perez, but his spare sleeping bag was unzipped and, as Gina put out a hand to reassure herself of his presence, she could still feel his warmth.

She got up, dressed only in the sweatshirt, and looked out of the tent warily. Perez was sitting alone. In the distance sat Caninde and Jeronimo. No sign of Sinon! Gina shuddered. What was she going to do about what had happened? The thought that she had been attacked was sickening. She tried to pull herself together. She wasn't going to let him get away with what he'd done. She'd see him pay for that as much as for trading skins!

Swallowing the bile in her throat, and gingerly feeling her sore lips, Gina went back inside to dress properly. Later, she joined Perez at his lonely breakfast. He turned to her. 'How do you feel now?' She sat beside him as Caninde handed her a bowl of hot steaming fish broth. She just stared at it and put it down. She had no appetite for food.

'Okay. I ache a bit, that's all. But he didn't do anything major. He just hurt me. I'll survive! Where is he, anyway?'

His mouth tightened. 'I'd call attempted rape *major*! And using a knife! He won't come back, I can tell you.' Perez put out his hand and took Gina's. As he chafed its coldness, he realised she was trembling. But Gina didn't respond in any other way, and Perez recognised both defiance and fear in her face.

Perez felt terrible, trapped by a strange fatalism. He blamed himself for the night before. What was happening to him? Was he a jinx on the women he loved? First, losing Dorita to the river, and now this savage attack on the girl who had come to mean something to him after he had been so long alone. He should have been with her. He should have stayed closer. How could he have gone off the way he had and left her open to so much risk? He'd known Sinon was a bad lot, but not a rapist! He looked at her, but she didn't speak; only the expression on her pale face said it all.

A moment later, she whispered, 'The trip is over. I want to go back.' The white face and the lovely blue, black-lashed eyes that he'd grown to love tugged at his heart. He reached out to touch a small bruise that had appeared on her cheekbone, and felt desperately angry when he saw the swelling on her lips.

He was crying inside too – he didn't blame her for wanting to call the trip off. 'Yes, I agree.'

She looked at him, her eyes pleading. 'You know I don't want to, but I have to.'

Not a muscle moved in his face. So it was over. He was doomed to be alone again. Once Gina got back to Belem, she wouldn't want the likes of him around. He had no chance, with a man like Mark Baxter for her to go back to. Someone who would give her the life she was born to; not a man like him, who'd left her alone to fight off the likes of Sinon. He put his bowl down and stood up, stroking a hand along her hair. 'You don't have to explain. You're calling the shots, remember?'

Gina was confused. Inside, she was begging Perez to tell her that everything was all right between them; that he cared about her in spite of Sinon. She wanted him to tell her that this trip needn't end this way. That he'd take care of her, protect her. That they would go on together without Sinon. But he didn't. He only nodded and pulled her to him quickly.

They stood together in silence for a moment, then he let her go. She had no way of knowing what he was feeling. Maybe he thought she had given the Greek the come on, invited him into her tent? Which she had, but quite innocently. She could have kicked herself for her stupidity. After all, how did he view one-night stands? Which was what they'd had – although it didn't feel like it ...

She felt broken-hearted! Mad thoughts came rushing ... Perhaps he felt nothing for her? Perhaps he believed it was her fault? But how could he? Maybe this was how all men behaved after something like that? Perhaps he felt ashamed? That was more like it. But one thing kept flashing on and off in her mind like a horrible warning signal. Had she been just a pleasant diversion for Perez? She could see Sinon's ugly face as he had suggested it. Maybe Perez really did like only Indian girls? Maybe he was disgusted by what had happened? Then remorse for thinking bad things about him overtook the madness. If only he'd say something. She only needed the tiniest hint that would show she was loved and trusted.

'How soon do you want to leave?' he asked, his face blank.

Gina answered bleakly. 'As soon as we can.'

'I'll get Caninde and Jeronimo to start packing,' he replied quietly, then walked away.

Later, as he helped stow the tents into the packs, Perez was wondering if it was the best thing after all. It soured his gut to think of her and Baxter. Perez straightened up, stretching his cramped arms from the rolling of the canvas. He felt very far from the lover he'd been with Gina in his arms. He looked across to where she was packing her things. Her face was in profile as she leaned over the pack, and Perez felt his heart bump as he watched her movements. He certainly felt for the girl.

The idea came to him suddenly and shocked him like an ice-cold shower. If she went home and he never saw her again, he would be bereft. He looked up at the sky and across the clearing, his mind soaring through the forests he loved. Another thing he knew, too: that the rainforests would mean nothing like they'd meant before, unless she was with him and loving them too.

10

'Lapotikee!'

The young warrior stopped playing his flute and looked toward Elena. It was still early, and a mist hung in the air. He got to his feet, his young, hard-muscled body showing no spare flesh. He stood, silent and immobile, waiting like a dark shadow. He was 17 and, in the Xingu, already a man; tall, with broad, muscled shoulders and long legs that tapered gracefully away from his firm, sharp-edged hips. His arms were folded across his chest, and his skin glistened dully in the moon's light.

The Greek girl walked over to him, her look strafing his body. 'Lapotikee, did you do as I asked?'

The young Indian's eyes burned into hers. He had quarrelled with his father about this woman. Tioti had been chosen as his wife. It would be irresponsible to ignore Santana's warning, but what could he do? Santana would not know; he was far away in the country of the Waura with the others. Besides, the white woman fascinated him. He had listened to the tales of the strangers when they had come to his village. He had heard of the women who were as fair as the sun.

This Elena was such a woman. To him, she was a goddess; the embodiment of the fire that gave him life; a priestess. If his father discovered his enslavement to a European woman, he would have to leave the village. He would be disgraced and no longer allowed his place as warrior champion. Sometimes, when he wanted her so much and could no longer stand the pain, he would chew on the dream paste that his father kept hidden in the house. The dream paste held magic powers; it helped him forget this Elena. He answered her slowly. 'I did as you asked.'

Elena stroked a hand along the smooth, brown skin of the Indian's chest, smiling as she felt the youth quiver at her touch. 'What did you see?'

'I saw many things.'

'Tell me what you saw.'

'I saw the English girl weeping.' Lapotikee's voice was cold, as though the memory was bad.

Elena lifted her dark eyes to his, making sure he didn't see she was angry. 'Because of Perez?'

The Indian looked over his shoulder furtively. 'No, your Greek man.'

Elena started to laugh. Lapotikee wasn't happy when she laughed like that; it was like she was making fun of him; but he had no way of knowing Elena's real thoughts.

But Elena was thinking how sweet was revenge! And even more sweet when it concerned another woman. So the old devil had tried it on with Gina? Well, it served her right! The laughter faded, and Lapotikee saw the ugly shadow cross her face again. She was thinking about herself and Sinon's profits, whether or not his deals had been successful.

She sat down on the carved wooden stool, picking up the boy's flute and blowing a few low notes through the mouthpiece. After a few moments, she put the flute down again. 'Tell me, Lapotikee,' she murmured, 'what else did you see?'

Lapotikee wished she wouldn't touch his flute. He wished, too, that she wouldn't call him by his name – it was forbidden; it meant that she owned his soul. But to touch the flute was worse. Usually, women were not meant even to see them. Only those who were near death, or gripped with the fever of a first-born son, were allowed, because the magic of their music pleased the gods on the other side of the world.

He looked over his shoulder again. 'I went with Sinon to the land of my brothers, beyond the river. They had many pelts for him this time, and some of the yellow stones they call gold.' Elena nodded. This sounded very promising. Lapotikee continued, 'Sinon spoke of men coming from Cachimbo with more money and dream dust. They come on the silver plane that flies like a bird above our heads. He told my father these men will carry much money. Money for ...' He stopped.

'Yes, I know. Money for your father.' She smiled up at him. 'He will have the means to buy many guns now, I think. You have done well, Lapotikee. Shall I reward you?' There was a teasing smile around her mouth.

'This night? A sheen of sweat glistened over the young brave's body, and his eyes had taken on an eager, hot look. 'In the House of Strangers?'

'In *your* house, Lapotikee. After moonrise! Then you can tell me everything,' she breathed.

He moistened his dark lips, his eyes on the rise and fall of her breasts through the thin shirt. He desired her more than anything; more, even, than the peace of his spirit. 'This time must be for more than mouth touches!' he said boldly. 'This time I want more.'

'And you shall have it, Lapotikee. I know you will please me.' She smiled into the Indian's dark eyes, which were glittering now at her promise. 'You've watched Sinon. You've followed your father. And now you've told me the English girl's troubles. You will be rewarded.'

He nodded with excitement.

'And, if you tell me when the plane is coming, there will be *everything* for you.' Elena was still smiling, but her eyes were like ice. It was vital now that she knew when the plane would land and, even more so, who would be on it. The boy mustn't let her down now. 'Do you understand? It is very important to me.'

'This night?' he repeated.

Elena nodded. 'After moonrise! Go on now. I will come to you later, when you send me the signal.'

Lapotikee nodded abruptly. Then, with a swift movement,

he turned and disappeared into his father's house. He was aching at the thought of the woman. And, in preparation, he had to give himself time to chew more of the magic paste.

Elena drew a hand across her damp forehead. If allowing Lapotikee to believe she would be his lover was the only way to bribe him, then she would. Soon she wouldn't need him anymore and she would have Perez, because she would have the real proof to send Sinon where he belonged – to jail! That document that he and the Chief had sworn was what she had to have at any cost. The young Indian's greed for money, his passion for her, had been insatiable, and he had been easily persuaded.

Elena smiled as she walked back to the House of Strangers. But the smile was still nervous. She had to be careful how she timed it. So far, so good! While Santana and Sinon had been cooking up their illegal plans for fortune, she had got down to her own. She had made it her business to bribe and cajole the chief's son. That way, she had been able to discover how much wealth Sinon had amassed in the Manaus warehouse; how much money had been exchanged for the animal skins and for the gold, panned by the illegal prospectors who ventured into the Xingu. And finally, the most damning evidence of all for Sinon, she had found out about the gun-running to the Indians.

The Indians used the money for drugs, too. She suspected that Santana was already a rich man, probably through cocaine and gold. And how long it would be before Sinon tired of trading only in pelts and turned completely to that dangerous trade was anybody's guess.

Elena swung herself into her hammock, her acquisitive brain ticking over. Blackmail could be very lucrative. Her fat lover would pay a great deal for her silence. That night she hoped to have in her grasp the proof that she needed. And, when she was armed with that amount of money, how could Rafe ignore her? The hammock swayed gently from side to side. Elena reflected that the fact that Lapotikee was hooked on the deadly dust made the prospects even brighter. He wouldn't ask for very much. She'd make sure of that!

She smiled to herself again. So Gina was in trouble, was she? No more than she deserved, after being stupid enough to go on an expedition like this! Elena lay back and rocked herself calmly.

Lapotikee waited until he caught sight of the girl with the moon-bright hair, then stole soundlessly through the silent *malocas*. He was sweating profusely. He was more than ready to mingle his blood with hers that night. He'd obeyed her without question, done all she'd asked, and now she had to pay.

That night was to be a celebration, and he had prepared himself carefully. He had marked his body to indicate his tribal rank, and around his neck hung his precious necklace of jaguar claws. And, as befitted the chief's son, he had painted his body into a rare and special pattern – the polka-dotted design of royal privilege. That night this woman would know the warrior Lapotikee. She would discover how much he knew about the heat of the hunter and his kill. What came between did not matter.

Elena gave a little gasp as his *ucuru*-daubed body suddenly barred her way. The moonlight glinted on the fine gold chain around her neck, and he took it between his fingers. He had seen symbols like this before, around the necks of the strangely-dressed women who came to the village from time to time and called themselves *Sisters*. Lapotikee had no sisters, and he frowned curiously at the tiny gold crucifix as he turned it around in his palm. 'Xingu women never wear this,' he said. 'Do you wear it for Lapotikee?'

'I wear it to please Elena.'

He let it drop back between her breasts. Then, taking her arm, he led her into his house. Elena made no sound as she passed through the reed-plaited doorway. Then Lapotikee was coming forward, slinking with the stealth of a jungle beast, pointing at the matted floor. She sat down coolly, but her heart was beating fast. Then he offered her the *epena*.

'No, Lapotikee, not for me! But more for you.' She knew too

well what it was, and no hallucinatory drug was going to impair her judgement. Lapotikee sniffed deeply from the thin tube as she watched. He believed the drug would give him peace! But as she watched the boy fill his nostrils with the stuff, she knew what it really did.

'Tell me, Lapotikee,' she whispered. 'No further until you do!'

He grinned, slurring his words. 'Cachimbo plane – in three more days. Men from over the great ocean. Bring much for our people and the white men living far beyond the river. Now you must keep your promise!' His heart lurched as the gold crucifix swung against his body. In a haze, he almost remembered his father's warning and the words of the old men of the village. His befuddled brain asked, *Was their Devil real? Was this really a woman who would hunt the heart out of a man?*

'Tell me more, Lapotikee. The men – the plane ...' She teased him and cajoled. 'Tell Elena. Come on. Do they always bring white dust when they come to see your father?'

'Yes. He takes it down the river and changes it for the animals' skins and the yellow stones. My father already has much of it. Look! I'll show you!' He slid a shaking hand under the reed mat and struggled to lift a flat stone, from beneath which he produced a leather pouch. 'Look, goddess! This is mine! Six ocelot for this!'

Elena stared at the rough cocaine paste. At last she knew, but still had no tangible proof! 'You've done well, Lapotikee, but I need more.'

'And I!' His half-closed eyes tried to focus.

'And more,' her voice was like music.

'My father also has paper. Do you wish to see?'

'Yes. Show me your father's paper.'

Lapotikee fumbled around, groping aimlessly until Elena helped him take out two sheets of folded paper. Her eyes gleamed as she skimmed the documents. The first was the contract signed personally between Sinon and Santana, giving an inventory of the deals they had made together, from the number of pelts sold to the amount of illegal gold. There was even a column giving the price of a kilo of cocaine. The second was a catalogue of arms suppliers and the amounts paid for the guns over the last six years. Elena smiled

'I have done well?' the youth asked.

Elena nodded. She reached over to fold the papers inside her bag, which lay on the floor. But Lapotikee grabbed them.

'No!'

'If I don't, then ...!' She was gambling he wouldn't last much longer.

'No more?'

'No more!' His red eyes probed hers. 'Your father will not miss them. And you will have them back.' It was risky, but it was a risk she had to take. 'I shall only take them for a while. You can trust me. You know that.'

'I have done well?'

'Yes, very well.'

He was muttering incoherently, trying to catch at her robe. It was only when he was no longer capable of thought or action that she stole the incriminating evidence and crept out of his house, after carefully replacing the stone and obliterating all signs of his or her hands.

Later, in the House of Strangers, she lay on her back in the hammock. A few moments later, she held up her little brandy flask, unscrewing the top and drinking deeply. She closed her eyes as the liquid started its warm glow in her belly, burning its way down and comforting her. What she had done had been entirely necessary. *And it has been worth it*, she thought, as she lay fingering the precious papers safe inside her money belt.

She was glad of the silence around her. She wanted to sleep and wash away the memory of the last few hours. Maybe even until the others came back. Three or four days of peace. All she had to do now was be patient.

It was a little before noon the next day when Elena heard the sounds in the clearing. She dragged herself up and walked to the door.

She couldn't believe it. Perez and the two Indians were coming toward her. Gina Matheson was walking behind them. Perez nodded and returned Elena's astonished gaze. 'We cut the trip short.'

She glanced from one to the other. 'Why? What's happened?'

He shrugged, moving nearer to the house. 'It's a long story.'

'Where's Sinon – and Santana?'

'I don't know.' He seemed past caring now, and passed by her to go into the house. Gina was already inside.

'I want to know,' Elena insisted.

'He'll turn up sooner or later, and right now I need a stiff drink.'

She followed him and grabbed his arm. 'Listen, Perez, I have something to tell you, and it's very important.'

'Not now, Elena!'

'You'll want to know! It's about Sinon and his deals.'

Perez stopped. 'Tell me.'

'Not now. I'll be by the river ...' She glanced over toward Gina and lowered her voice. 'It will be best for her if *she* doesn't know when. Listen.' She stretched up and whispered something. Perez stared at her, then nodded. A moment later, he left her and strode through into the wash-room.

Elena walked over to Gina, who'd been watching the two of them. 'What happened out there? she asked. 'He looks mad enough to kill someone.'

Gina was utterly determined that Elena would find out nothing about the ill-fated excursion. She smiled ruefully and said, her voice a little strained and remote, 'We're all very tired; it's been a bad trip.'

'What's gone wrong? What's happened to Sinon?'

'Don't ask me, ask Perez! I'm tired!'

Gina excused herself. She could hear Perez moving about as he sloshed the water over him. She flopped down into her hammock. What a mess! She lay listening as he moved about behind the reed partition, and wondered. The atmosphere between the two of them was still there. And he had been letting Elena whisper something to him. She couldn't bear to think it might have concerned her.

He still had not spoken about how he felt. On the way back, he'd been kind and considerate, so different from when they'd first met, but he'd kept his distance. Was he waiting for some form of gesture from her? Was he waiting for an explanation? Or had he been playing with her all along, and now that the trip was almost over, regretting making love to a client? Gina closed her eyes wearily. Surely he still cared for her?

In spite of the agonising, she was soon asleep, and when Perez came back into the room, he covered her sleeping form with the mosquito net. He looked down at her face. Her arm was thrown above her head at an uncomfortable angle, and he brought it down gently by her side. He frowned. He had no idea why he was so attracted to her. He had never cared much for European women. But Gina was different. Perhaps it was because he didn't have to put on an act with her – as if they'd known each other for years. This feeling in himself that he mustn't touch her again was becoming unbearable.

He grimaced. Something would have to be done about Sinon, who was a dangerous and foul man in more ways then one, and who wouldn't think twice about going for Gina again if he got a chance. One way or another, Perez would have his work cut out until they were safely back in Belem. Perhaps he should call it a day and fetch in Fred with the chopper? But what did Elena know? He was going to meet her, even though he didn't want to …

Elena lay in her hammock and watched Perez standing over the English girl. Her jealous heart beat very fast. She would have liked to have jumped up there and then and made her feelings known, but she didn't. She kept playing for time and the big scene she was planning. At least Perez had been interested. She had known he would be. But what had happened to Sinon? He must have pushed his luck with the Matheson girl. And the look on Perez's face as he prepared his hammock told Elena it was better to keep her mouth shut. Inside, she knew that he would keep his promise to her!

Sinon came back to the settlement during the night. Instead of going into the House of Strangers to risk another beating from Perez, he took up Santana's offer and rested in the house of the chief. He wouldn't have come back at all if he'd had a choice. As it was, he'd trekked for two days through the deep forests solely for the sake of Santana, who was becoming greedy. Without the guns, there would be no skins.

And, to complete his deal with the Portuguese arms dealer, Sinon had been forced to avoid the easier route in case he ran into Perez again. If Perez ever knew about the gun-running, then it could spell disaster. It was bad enough having him as an enemy over the girl. It would be the end for Sinon if he knew of the shipments as well.

When Elena saw Sinon in the clearing next morning, she wasted no time. 'I've missed you, Sinon.'

At the sound of the girl's voice, Sinon turned, greeting her and cupping her chin. He reflected wryly on her remarkable ability to lie. 'Did you, my sweet?'

'You know I did. Come and sit here by me,' Elena smiled. She led him away from Santana's, and they sat down by the lorry. 'Tell me why you didn't come back with the others. What happened out there?'

The Greek lifted a cynical eyebrow. 'Were you worried about me?'

'Of course I was.'

He laughed softly. 'It was just a misunderstanding. The English girl decided to cut the trip short.'

She eyed him directly, reaching out to touch his cheekbone. 'Is that how you got these?'

He jerked his bruised face away from her touch, anger showing bright in his puffed-up eyes. 'Leave it alone. It is nothing.'

In the privacy of the forest, Lapotikee stood limply in front of his father, Santana, who had found his papers gone. It was then he was made to promise that the Greek woman would never get away with them.

That evening, Elena waited for Perez. She was sure he would come and appreciate all she had done, and see how beautiful she had made herself for him. She started at the shrill cry of a harpy eagle and looked round, half afraid in case it was Lapotikee. But no-one was to be seen, and she felt relieved. And the dark shape, its face hidden by a frightening mask, slid behind the trees, out of her sight, and waited to listen to her conversation with Perez …

'What do you want, Elena? Why all the secrecy?' Perez faced her. 'What's so important that it couldn't be said in front of the others?'

She looked at him from under her lashes. 'I have news that will change things for us.'

'Change things in what way? And what do you mean, *us*?'

'You must help me.'

'Why must I?'

Elena moved forward, slipping her arms round his neck. 'We can have everything, Perez. I'll soon possess the means to keep you in comfort for the rest of your life.'

He dragged her arms down. 'What the hell are you talking about?'

'I've found out things. I have the proof that Sinon is not only dealing in skins, but guns for the Indians too. Not only that, he's dealing in gold and cocaine as well. Once I have it out with him, he'll have to pay me for my silence. Just think, Perez, how much money he'll have to pay for *this*.'

Perez stared through narrowed eyes at the papers Elena was now holding up in her hand. He'd known about the pelts, of course, and had guessed about the cocaine. So, Sinon's deadly game involved gun-running, too. He'd always suspected it, but had never been able to prove it! 'Mother of God,' he muttered harshly. 'If this is true, he's finished. What's in those papers? Where did you get them?'

'It's true.' Elena's heart was beating so fast she was sure he could hear it. She could see that Perez was hooked on the idea. 'Sinon doesn't stand a chance now, nor Santana. I got the evidence from that brat Lapotikee, last night.'

She paused, smiling up at him cautiously and pushing the papers back into her money belt. 'I did this for you, my darling, *and me*, of course – but before I show them to you, I want you to promise something.'

Perez's frown deepened. 'What?'

'That you give up the English girl and come back to me.'

Perez's flesh crawled. He stared at her, his expression reflecting no trace of his disgust. 'And if I don't?'

She held his gaze, her expression cold and ruthless. 'It'd be very easy for me to add your name to Sinon's.'

Perez smiled faintly. Blackmail, then? He was in no doubt that Elena meant what she said. And that she was right about what Sinon was up to.

Gun-running was one the things Perez hated the most, along with the slums of Manaus and Brasilia; the rainforest's destruction; the misery of the addicts; and the killing of the jungle's beautiful creatures. But he knew how unscrupulous Elena was. She would think nothing of adding his name to the damning evidence if she couldn't have her way. He had to be cautious. He answered calmly. 'I thought the idea was to blackmail Sinon, not me.'

'We could be so happy, Perez.'

'What's your plan?'

'I'll threaten Sinon.' Her hand was on the belt. 'Then I'll tell him that unless he pays me enough, I'll hand the papers over to the authorities. Anyway, I've made my plans, nothing *can* go wrong. And when he gives me the cash, I'll meet you in Belem. Then we can go away.'

'And when do you intend to put this plan into action?'

She smiled archly. 'Not just yet. Lapotikee told me when a plane is due from Cachimbo, and on board will be two men –

Sinon's contacts. We don't want him to get wind of anything until we have them, too. They're bringing the rest of the cash.' Elena waited expectantly. 'Well, Perez, what do you say?'

Pity for the girl touched Perez briefly; she was playing one hell of a dangerous game. But, for now, he'd go along with it – until he had in his own hands the proof that was going to put Sinon inside, where he belonged. Only that way would the forest rid itself of the evil of these men. Sinon was not getting away with what he'd done to Gina!

'Okay, I agree,' he said quietly. 'But, for your own safety, you'd better let *me* keep the papers.'

The Greek girl laughed softly. 'Oh no, Perez. You can have the papers *when I say*. I'm calling the shots.'

'What's going to happen if Sinon finds out?'

'He won't. And you won't be messing round with the English girl anymore?'

He nodded, playing for time.

'Okay, it's a deal.' Elena sighed her relief. She looked up into his face and put her arms around him again. 'Now, Perez, kiss me before we go.'

He bent forward reluctantly, planting his cold lips against her eager ones.

She tried to open his mouth with her tongue, but she couldn't. 'You're so cold, Perez,' she said. 'But I'll warm you up when we're back in Belem.'

He straightened up, pulling her arms down. 'I'm tired, Elena. Go back to the house on your own, and I'll see you in the morning.'

She glanced at him, surprised. 'In the morning? Aren't you staying in the House of Strangers?'

'No. I'm with Caninde and Jeronimo tonight.'

She shrugged lightly. 'Okay. Anyway, I don't want you near the English girl now you're mine.'

Perez watched her walk away, conscious of the triumph in the girl's eyes as she'd kissed him. But he knew he would never touch Elena again.

The Greek girl crossed the sleeping commune to the House

of Strangers, exultant that her intuition had been right all along. Inside, she walked over and stared into Gina's sleeping face. She could see the trace of bruises! But she wasn't sorry one bit. How she'd love to waken her and tell her that Perez was hers, and hers only.

In the small hours of the morning no-one noticed the chief's son, Lapotikee, enter his father's house and arouse the sleeping Sinon. Nor did they see the dark and stealthy forms creep into the House of Strangers a little while later ...

When morning came, Gina woke up to find herself on her own. She stretched lazily first, then looked around. She got up and saw that Elena's hammock was empty. She knew the Greek girl wasn't noted for early rising, so she went to investigate. But there was nothing near the hammock to show Elena had ever existed. Her bag and all her paraphernalia had disappeared. Nothing to show that the girl had been there at all. Except ... Gina stooped hesitantly to pick up the broken chain that had once held the tiny Christian cross around Elena's neck. She hadn't heard a sound! But, while she'd slept, Elena had disappeared. She was alone in the House of Strangers. The only movement came from the vacillating, oblong shaft of sunlight that lightened the doorway. Gina looked across the empty, echoing space and ran outside in a panic.

11

Perez felt his gut tighten when he saw the way Gina rushed out of the house. His dark eyes were anxious as he caught sight of her pale, confused face.

He strode toward her. 'What's wrong?'

Gina opened her palm to show Perez the broken chain. 'Perez! I found this by Elena's hammock. It's her chain. She wears it all the time – she would never have taken it off herself.' She reached out to grip his arm. 'Perez! She gone. I have a horrible feeling something awful has happened to her.'

Perez took the chain from Gina and studied it closely. His face was grim and taut. 'You may be right,' he replied. 'She never takes this off.'

Gina's frightened grip on his arm tightened, and he swore silently as her lovely eyes searched his face, bright darts of fear betraying her alarm. His own dark ones flickered back to the chain, fearing the worst, and he hesitated – just fractionally – before he muttered, 'Okay, show me.'

They went back into the House of Strangers. He should have known better than to meet Elena the night before. He was full of loathing for her, but he wouldn't like to think she'd been hurt. It was more likely that Sinon had her holed up somewhere. He was sickened by the surge of disgust and loathing he felt for the Greek. He was in no doubt that this was his doing; that he had had a hand in whatever had happened to Elena. No way would Sinon want her tale-telling.

He could only think that someone must have overheard their conversation the night before, when they had met on the river bank; but who that someone could be was beyond him. He knew it couldn't have been Sinon personally, because he'd made sure the Greek was safely with Santana before he'd set out to meet Elena. Probably one of his spies. He swore under his breath. *You crazy, little fool, Elena. Did you think for one minute you'd get away with it?* His brain was already computing where the natives might have taken her. She wouldn't be in the village. Maybe some spot in the forest? He thought hard ...

Gina glanced quickly up at him, her blue eyes bright through the dimness. 'Do you know something about this, Perez?'

He stared at her for a moment, then bent forward and, to her surprise, took her in his arms and allowed his lips to brush lightly against her cheek. He could feel her tenseness. 'Not personally, Gina, but I'm going to find out, and until then, we have to watch every step we take from now on, my darling.'

Her arms went around his neck, holding on to him tightly to give herself further reassurance. 'Hold me, Perez. Please, hold me. I'm scared.'

For several minutes he cuddled her, neither of them saying a word. And when at last they broke away, Perez read in Gina's eyes the thing he had been waiting so long to see. Trust.

'Gina,' he said, 'I'm so sorry about what happened with Sinon.' He hid his tanned face against her blonde hair. He had never felt so protective of any woman as he did at that moment, not even Dorita. Love was the last thing he should have been bothering with then. But he couldn't help it.

'I know. It's okay!'

He withdrew. 'If only I could make it up to you properly. But I can't now. I have to go after Elena. Do you understand?'

'Of course. I can't bear to think what's happened!' Gina didn't like the girl, but she'd never wished her any harm. 'But – what do you mean by *properly*?' She knew she was being selfish, holding him up, but she had to know where they stood.

He smiled, in spite of his anxiety. Only a woman could ask a question like that at such a time! 'I'm not used to explaining things, Gina, but I think you know what I mean.'

She shook her head. 'Perez, are you trying to tell me that if we weren't in this mess over Elena, you'd like nothing better than to make love to me again?'

He pulled her into his arms. 'Gina, my guts ache every time I look at you. But it's more than that. My feelings for you go further than a roll in the forest.'

'How far, Perez?'

'As far as any man's can for a woman.'

There was a brief pause. Then she looked up at him. 'Are you – are you telling me you *love* me, Perez?'

He hesitated. He'd never told anyone that before. Then he smiled. 'Yes, I suppose I am.' He only hoped he hadn't ruined his chances with her now, and he waited for the response that was sure to come – one way or the other!

He loved her! She was stunned for a moment. Then she was reaching up to kiss him and acknowledging her own feelings. 'I guess I love you, too, Perez.'

'I didn't want to frighten you. To push you.'

'*You* could never frighten me.'

'After what Sinon did to you, I ...'

Gina put a hand over his mouth. 'Shh, that's done with. He isn't worth even thinking about.'

'No.' He pushed back her hair until he could see all of her face. He could have stared at her forever. Then he broke away. 'This is crazy, Gina. I have to go. But before ...' He stopped. Then began again, 'Oh, hell, I know this is not the place, nor the appropriate time. But will you ...?' Perez broke off awkwardly, as though suddenly changing his mind and deciding to keep his leaping hopes to himself.

Gina prompted. 'Will I what?' She looked up at him, instinct telling her that, in spite of all the terrible things that were happening around them, this was probably going to be the most wonderful moment of her life. She waited expectantly as he held her to him. 'Will I what, Perez?' she asked again.

'Will you ...?' He looked down and swallowed. 'How do you

feel about staying with me and ...' He stopped, trying to gauge the look in her eyes. To gain the courage. He looked down at Elena's chain. 'I can't guarantee it'll be happy ever after, but I'll give it a damn good try. That's if you will. And – if you don't let me go now, there mightn't be the chance!' She gasped at the words.

They broke apart, and Perez was reaching into the pocket of his jeans to take something out. 'Hang on, you'd better take this.' He pressed the cold, hard object into her hand, and when Gina looked down, her smile froze as she saw the pistol.

'What's this for?'

'I want you to do exactly as I say. If it becomes necessary, use it.'

'Necessary?'

'It's in case anyone tries to harm you when I'm not around.'

She looked blankly at the gun. 'But I don't know how. I've never used one before.' She stopped, breathed in and said, 'I'd be a lousy shot.'

'No you wouldn't. It's easy.' He took the revolver from her nervous hand. 'Look, see this?' He pointed to the safety catch. 'Just slip it like this, and the bullet is ready. All you have to do then is point it and squeeze the trigger. Got it?'

Her eyes were wide and dilated as she stared at the gun. 'I ... I think so.'

He pressed the gun back into her reluctant hand. 'Don't worry, if your life's in danger, you'll be Annie Oakley.' There was a snap in his voice now as he gripped her arms tightly, his face grave. 'Gina, promise me you'll use it if necessary.'

'If you say so.'

'I do.'

She nodded vigorously. 'Then I will. I promise.'

'I don't want to leave you, Gina, but I have no choice. I have to find out what's happened to Elena. The gun is a precaution, that's all.'

She nodded again. 'Okay. I understand. But can't I come with you?'

He drew her toward him again, holding her tight. 'That's

impossible. You must stay here. Better still, stay in the house of Luis' father, and I'll leave Jeronimo here as well.' He bent to kiss her quickly on the cheek. 'Try not to worry, I'll be back as soon as I can. In the meantime, try and have a rest? That way, the time will soon pass, and I'll be back before you know it.'

Gina shook her head. 'I have sleep coming out of my ears. I don't need any more. And, anyway,' she was looking at Elena's hammock fearfully, 'I'm frightened they'll come back for me.' When she saw the look on his face, she was sorry she'd said it. 'Don't take any notice, Perez. Don't worry about me. I'll be all right with Luis' family. I'll catch up on my notes. I haven't written anything up for ages.'

'Okay.' His voice was barely audible. 'Come on, let me take you over to Luis' house.' He kissed her again, and it comforted her a little.

Perez signalled for Jeronimo and made sure the Indian understood, speaking to him rapidly in his dialect. Then, not able to discover the whereabouts of either Sinon or Santana, they went into the *maloca* of Luis' family to leave Gina there.

Perez held her to him again before leaving her alone with the Indians. She seemed calmer now, her nerves controlled. 'Are you okay?'

She glanced at him sharply. 'Are you kidding?'

He smiled, a touch of relief lighting his eyes. That tiny flash of irritation told him she would be able to handle herself if she needed to. He pecked her cheek. 'I'll see you later.'

Perez returned to his house to prepare the search for Elena, feeling the tension growing within him as he loaded his rifle and checked his handgun. He knew that Santana's small army of Indians were well armed, but he knew also that they were amateurs, who were more accustomed to a spear than an automatic weapon. And, like most professionals, he was nervous. He knew nothing could be more dangerous than a gun in the hands of an amateur. He stood up, checking the rifle's telescopic sights once again, and was satisfied. He looked over to the Indian. 'Ready?'

Caninde looked back expressionlessly. 'Ready.'

Perez stuffed some spare ammunition into his pocket and buckled on his shoulder-holster. Looking up, he gave a brief nod to Caninde, and the two men went outside.

He looked across to where Santana's Indians were guarding the pelts. There was a possibility that Elena's body had been secreted underneath them. If she had been alive when they put her there, then she wouldn't be for long in this heat. Maybe she'd been taken to some outlying hut, but where? Would Sinon have gone as far as killing her? It all depended on his mood. He and Elena had been together a long time, and he was a very nasty customer, so he likely had other plans for dealing with her. Perez shut his eyes at the thought. There were worse things than dying!

If he were to try to search, he and his two Indians would have to take on half the tribe, who were well armed. And he had to consider Gina, who'd be caught in the crossfire. He decided it was a huge gamble that he wasn't prepared to take.

If he had been trying to get rid of Elena, he'd have made for the river. As for Gina ... he couldn't bear thinking about it. She had been made his responsibility, and now he loved her! Simple as that. Then the Indian was beckoning him.

'Come, look!' He disappeared into the undergrowth. Perez knew Caninde had found a trail. All at once, he remembered the isolated thatched hut where the fishermen pulled in the dugouts at night. It would be the ideal place to get Elena out of the way until they moved out. A woman would not survive a night if she had been dumped in the forest.

As they moved out of the clearing, a pair of dark eyes followed them, peering from between the plaited grass walls of the chief's house.

Sinon nodded in satisfaction as he heard Santana's quiet murmur, 'He's making for the river.' His plan had worked. He had outsmarted Perez, who was heading in the wrong direction! Sinon was too clever for him. Elena had been tied up and gagged and now lay in a hut on the fringe of the village, under the care of some Indians. She had underestimated Sinon, but he would leave her there for only a short while, to teach her a lesson. He didn't want her dead. Yet. The Greek's flabby lips broke into a satisfied smile. 'Good. Let's make sure that's where he stays.'

'My men laid a good trail. They are everywhere. They will obey me. Perez will not see another day. And my son is eager for forgiveness.' Santana had been very angry with the boy.

Sinon nodded again, a sullen, brooding anger burning within him. Lapotikee had done well to tell him of Elena's treachery the night before. Now she was safely out of the way, Perez must be silenced; he was the only one left who knew of Sinon's secret. Perez had closed his eyes to a lot of Sinon's business, but that was only because he'd had no proof. Now he had that proof! About the pelts! And the gun-running too!

Elena must have given him the papers. They were no longer in the House of Strangers. Had she wanted Perez that much? His eyes narrowed. Too bad for the guide. He had become as greedy as Elena. Perez was no fool, and Sinon was sure that he would have concealed the papers somewhere on his person, which was the safest place to keep them. His dead body would yield the evidence for sure.

He glanced up at the Indian chief. 'I want Elena to pay in my way, not yours. When she is back in Belem, I shall deal with her. She will never betray anyone again.'

'And will you leave the other woman here? I could find many uses for her!'

Sinon glared at the Indian. 'You have women of your own. Keep your hands off her. Her father is an important man. He has influence. He would have the village swarming with the military within days.' He eyed the Indian chief narrowly.

Sinon was now planning what to do about Gina, in view of what had passed between them. He had several ideas, like dumping her on some forest track to make her own way home. Besides, she still owed him a little fun. By the time she was found by her doting father – if ever – he would be far away, courtesy of his gun-running contacts – and certainly not in

Belem. Sinon carefully lit a cheroot. He continued sourly, 'You must control your people.'

'They have not yet learned the ways of your civilisation,' the chief returned, equally sourly.

Simon inhaled. He hated inefficiency. Although the chief had been of great value, he had not succeeded in winning over all the Indians of his tribe. Many didn't trust him. They could not understand why he needed so much of the white man's wealth, nor how he came by it. Nor did they approve of the way he had now possessed the land given to him by the white man's laws in payment for the yellow stones. Land that was left to them by right. A legacy of their ancestors. They didn't like his ways, and were already suspicious of his ambitions. If Santana wasn't careful, his own people could make trouble for him. The Greek pursed his thick lips. The Indian was beginning to be a nuisance. He would have to find some way of dispensing with him too. He smiled to himself.

'We have our customs, Greek,' the Indian reminded him. 'And you may change your mind about the English woman when Perez is out of the way.'

'I doubt it,' snarled Sinon.

'But you will owe me for his death. For our excellence in laying false trails. Perez is following them already. Why should *I* not have what you have had already?'

The two men stared at each other. *So, Santana knows about my little episode with Gina,* thought Sinon. *There are always traitors amongst us.* The chief was as dangerous as he was, but this time Sinon had the advantage. Without him, the Indians would not get their guns. It was a cat and mouse game, as it had always been, and the most wily would win. Sinon knew he was the best. Santana's savagery was no match for his cool reasoning.

There was no doubt that Perez would find the false trail laid the night before. He was far too good a guide to miss their tracks. He would probably believe that Elena had been thrown in the river. 'Perez is a hunter, Santana. He will know the signs.'

'And we will follow his.'

Sinon Demetrios smiled again, thinking silently to himself,

Well, Perez, my brave and foolish friend, at least you'll have one thing to thank old Sinon for! You will soon be reunited with your beautiful Dorita!

Perez and Caninde ranged stealthily along the banks of the river's tributary. Above them, following their every step, hung an insect cloud, the mosquitoes hungry and ferocious, causing Perez to brush them away continuously, glad of the khaki shirt that protected him. He grinned ruefully, noticing that the insects didn't seem to touch the Indian as he moved silently on in front. Caninde was left untroubled, pausing now and then to point to a fresh break in the brush land, indicating yet another human trace.

The undergrowth grew even more dense as they penetrated the forest. More than once the Indian was forced to reach into the home-made sheath of hide tied around his waist, and slash away at the choking foliage that was forever around them.

They were following the river now, veering away a little into the blackness of the trees. Sensing danger, Perez kept his hand hovering close to the gun in its holster around his hip. He thought of Gina. The tiny pistol he'd left her with was really no protection. It was merely a little popgun that would be useless at more than ten yards. Still, it was better than nothing, he supposed, but he prayed this thing would be over before she risked any more harm from Sinon. He hoped, too, that they might find Elena alive. But that was already becoming a faint hope.

Suddenly, Caninde stopped, turning back to Perez and pointing to an opening in the undergrowth. The Indian's face was filled with concern. 'Not good,' he whispered hoarsely. 'Look!' Perez caught him up, and spotted the sinister shred of white cotton that was clinging limply to the liana.

They moved in closer. Here, the undergrowth was trampled, broken all around, and as Perez moved nearer to the strip of cloth, he grew even more wary. He picked it off the liana, and his worst fears were confirmed. He recognised the material as coming from the dress Elena had worn when she'd been at the clearing with him the night before. 'Come on,' he muttered harshly. 'Let's see what's down here.'

They moved on, looking for more signs. The track was leading them down toward the deep basin where the river lay. The roughened tree trunks thinned out as they neared the quiet backwater, and Perez's gut feeling that they were not alone grew stronger by the minute. He knew only too well that if his suspicions were right, Santana and Sinon would have sent their scouts out long ago, and they were probably already surrounded, their every step marked as they went along.

They were close to the river now, and the backwater widened out, choked with under-brush. It was getting impossible to go any further, and as they reached the river's bank, a coldness grew inside Perez. But he was still hoping when the hut came in sight.

'Look, Perez!' Caninde called. He was holding up a small golden cross. 'This belong to Greek woman. Maybe she in the hut.'

'Maybe.' Perez's heart was thumping. A moment later, they were skirting the hut at a distance. It was the ideal place for an ambush! But all was still. He felt sure Elena was not alive.

'I go,' said Caninde.

'No,' Perez ordered. The Indian retreated. Perez threw a stone and, in the screaming of the startled forest birds and animals, sprinted out of the undergrowth and leaned against the wall of the hut. It was now or never. If the Indians were watching, this was when they would attack. But all was silence. He crept to the opening.

Inside, it was musty and dark. No body. No Elena. But on the floor lay a heap of white. Her dress! No matter how shallow and scheming Elena had been in her short life, she deserved better than the callous death she'd endured. He didn't want to think about her being thrown in the river ...

With a grim face, he retreated. Caninde didn't speak, but his eyes showed what Perez was thinking. Then he said, 'Could it be a false trail?'

'We can only hope. Come on.' He took the small cross from the Indian and pushed it into his pocket. 'Let's get back.' They turned and retraced their steps, their search over.

Five minutes later, the forest was crackling with the sound of gunfire, and Perez and Caninde were sliding quickly back into the thick cover of the trees, ducking their heads as the sound of rifle shots cracked around them. They both knew instinctively that they would be dead men if they came within range of the waiting Indians' sights.

'Santana's men?' The question hissed from Caninde.

'Seems so,' Perez replied in an undertone. 'Watch your back! Come on, this way! They're not turning us into an alligator's supper yet!'

They edged along between the foliage, both of them as silent as any forest creature. It was vital now that they got to the Indians before the Indians got to them.

Lapotikee listened for the sound of Perez. He needed this man dead. Only by taking his body back to the village would he gain his father's forgiveness. He had almost had him once, and had fired, but Perez had heard him, and he was as good at hunting as any Indian. And soon the light would be gone, and there would be no chance then.

Then, all at once, a shaft of light betrayed Perez. For one brief moment, the man stood in full sight of him, waiting for his companion. Lapotikee trained his gun, his hand steady. He took aim and squeezed the trigger; and as his gun spoke, the bullet sped toward Perez. Exultant, the young Indian leapt up from his hiding place. Suddenly, he saw a bright flash of light from Perez's direction and heard a loud whistling noise as another bullet sang. Then there was a silence, and golden shadows darkened his eyes. Lapotikee felt the heat in his face and heard the roaring in his ears. His hand felt numb, and the gun slipped away. He fell over backwards into the dense undergrowth.

Perez had been hoping to escape before anyone died. He froze for a moment, thankful that his assailant's aim had been less true than his own. Then he jerked into action, and he and Caninde fled through the forest as the others made their pursuit. And Perez knew there was no way he could risk going back to the settlement now. He had recognised his assailant: Chief Santana's son! Once the Indians told Santana what had happened, Perez was finished.

There was only one way out of this, and that was by the river. Somehow, they had to get out of the Xingu. They had to reach the airstrip, where they would be safe. But the only way out was by going upriver, then crossing the country of the Waura. And, before he did any of that, he needed to rescue Gina too – and fast!

12

Gina put down her ball-point and stretched her legs, thinking, in spite of everything, how good it would be to sit in a chair again. She pushed back her hair, glancing around the *maloca* and smiling affectionately at the remaining members of the four families who shared it.

As usual, the younger men had gone off hunting; all except Luis' father, Malakiyaua, who was keeping his promise to Perez and, with Jeronimo's help, was watching over Gina. They had treated her well, their hospitality effusive, if sometimes a little bizarre.

As soon as Perez had gone, and as was their custom, they had given her food. Expecting cassava as usual, and finding that it was not, Gina had nibbled warily on the strange concoction. It wasn't until later that she had discovered what it was, and the thought of it almost choked her. The little crispy things had been fried cicada! Surprisingly, they had been quite delicious. They had reminded her of scampi; and, so far at least, she had suffered no ill effects.

And a little while ago, in an effort to repay their hospitality and show her appreciation, Gina had put aside her writing and rashly tried her hand at the chores. It had been a mistake! Her efforts had been doomed from the start! Taking over at the loom, she had tried to knot the threads around the palm-leaf fibre, but hammock-weaving was definitely not her style. Her fingers had turned out to be about as useful as ten sore thumbs.

It had been a bad day for her confidence in other ways too! Determined to please, she had tried something else. In a rash moment of broodiness, she had offered to bath Luis' little sister, Kayanaku, explaining to the young Indian mothers the European way of doing it. That had been her second mistake!

To their intense amusement, Gina had immersed the child in a gourd of water, keenly aware of the barely-suppressed laughter at her back. Kayanaku had eyed Gina with a rather jaundiced air, howling her disapproval and struggling in Gina's arms like a floundering fish.

In the end, the child's mother, quietly and, Gina thought, rather smugly, had taken Kayanaku from her, submitting her to a cold shower from the more customary calabash shell. After that, when the fascinated giggles of the Indian women had subsided and peace had been restored, Gina had accepted the fact that perhaps these gentle women were not yet ready for Mothercare.

She had also accepted the fact that she was not one of them and never would be. And that as far as they were concerned, she might just as well be a creature from another planet. Gina had finally abandoned her efforts and returned to her notes, probably to her hosts' relief.

Yet in spite of all her catastrophes, and also what was going on in the camp, they still seemed bent on pleasing her. Gina was flattered and grateful. But, a little later, after the ordeal of the bath and the experience of the fried cicadas, her gratitude took a sudden downturn.

In a mixture of Portuguese and sign language, the Indian women told her of their wish to make her an honorary member of their tribe; and, for a short time, Gina responded eagerly to the compliment. However, on learning what it entailed, she decided she had to draw the line, and declined some of the strange ritual of hair plucking. Then she glanced at her watch again, worrying about Perez. It was long past midday. Surely he couldn't be much longer! With a small frown, she turned to her notes, her mind wandering back to the commotion outside the *maloca* less than an hour earlier.

Gina had stood beside Jeronimo and Malakiyaua, watching a small group of weary Indians carry the lifeless body of the chief's son, Lapotikee, back into the village. Instinctively she had known that this new tragedy boded more ill for them – and that Perez was somehow involved.

She turned back to her work, trying hard to concentrate, but a few moments later she glanced up again, disturbed by the swift movement of Jeronimo as he leaped up to stand beside Malakiyaua at the door.

A notch of fear twisted her stomach when she heard Sinon's voice come from outside the house. She stood up quickly, moving to stand behind the Indians as they barred the Greek's entry into the *maloca*. She and Sinon hadn't made contact since the ugly incident in her forest tent, and she didn't want to!

'What is it? What do you want, Sinon?' she asked quietly, her hand clasped tightly around the small gun in her pocket.

'Will you tell these Indians to get out of my way? I have news for you about Perez.'

'What news? What about Perez?'

'Will you allow me to enter? It's very difficult talking to you like this.'

She glanced quickly at Jeronimo. 'It's all right, let him in.'

'Perez say on no account you speak to Greek.'

'I know, Jeronimo. But he has news of him. We must hear it.'

The Indian guide and Luis' father exchanged glances. They muttered something that Gina could not understand, then stood to one side, allowing passage for the Greek but barring contact, as they crossed spears between him and Gina. Jeronimo stared at him coldly, warning, 'You speak to the lady, Greek. But you do not touch her.'

'I have no intention of touching her.' Sinon took a couple of steps inside the *maloca* and regarded Gina warily. 'I see you are well protected.'

'Yes, I am, Sinon. Perez made sure of that.'

The Greek smiled softly, shaking his head. 'Poor Perez. I have bad news of Perez, little one. His protection is of nothing now.'

Gina froze, her eyes wide and staring at the Greek. 'What are you saying, Sinon?'

'Early this morning, he went out to look for Elena.'

'I know that! Where is she, Sinon? What have you done to her?'

'Why should I have done anything to her?'

'But we know damn well that you have, Sinon. When I woke up this morning and saw the state of the house, I knew *something* must have happened to her. We all know it has!'

'Nonsense, little one. You know what a strange creature Elena is. She is fond of the wild animals – especially the ones with two legs. Perhaps she is having a little fun with one or two of them now, eh?'

'For God's sake, Sinon! Do you think I'm completely off my head? I know something's happened to her! Is it because she's found out at last how you make your money?'

'What nonsense you talk. What's wrong with the way I make my money?'

Gina stared at him with scorn. 'We all know about your filthy trade!'

He smiled coldly. 'Come, come, little one. It is not as *filthy* as you say. It's a good business. Beautiful women pay well to have the feel of fur upon their skin.'

'Never mind that, Sinon,' she gritted, feeling sick with disgust, yet a desperate fear gnawing at her now. 'What news of Perez?'

He smiled again, taking a step forward, but stopping abruptly as the Indians barred his way. He sighed, shrugging. 'I fear it is bad – the worst.'

Gina froze. 'How bad?'

'Santana's men brought back the body of Lapotikee a little while ago. '

'I know. I saw, and I'm sorry.'

'The hand that killed him belonged to Perez, and I'm afraid he won't be coming back to you now.'

She stared at the Greek uncertainly, the fear growing even stronger. 'What the hell are you saying?'

'I'm saying that the Indians do not like the death of Santana's son. It is their duty to avenge such an act, and so it is impossible that your friend is still alive.' He paused, his eyes cold and ruthless, continuing softly, 'There is only me now, Gina. Only I can get you home safely. Perhaps you won't pour such scorn on Sinon now.' He turned away, laughing softly.

Stunned and fearful, Gina watched him walk back to the house of Santana. 'You're a liar!' she called despairingly to his disappearing bulk. 'Perez will be back! I don't believe a word you say!'

He turned again to her briefly, still smiling. 'It is unimportant whether you believe me or not, little one. I have told you the truth.'

Gina stood motionless as she watched the Greek enter Santana's house, loneliness and despair overwhelming her, She was afraid. She glanced quickly at Jeronimo, who had heard it all. 'Do you believe him, Jeronimo?'

The Indian was frowning. 'That Perez killed Lapotikee may be the truth. But that the others kill Perez, I do not believe. He and my brother, Caninde, are too good for Santana's men. We must wait for them here as he told us.'

Wearily, Gina turned back into the house and placed the revolver gingerly on top of her scattered pile of notes. There was nothing she could do except as Jeronimo said. But when sunset came and Perez still hadn't returned, Gina's desperation had almost reached fever-pitch. She felt so helpless waiting around, able to do nothing, and her thoughts flew longingly to the radio at the airstrip. She passed a little time mentally devising ways and means of getting there with only Jeronimo as guide, but it was an impossible preoccupation. Jeronimo rejected all her suggestions instantly, dismissing them as the impracticalities they were. Gina lived through the longest 24 hours of her life; and, as the day burned itself out, she prayed for Perez's safe return.

'Don't you think we ought at least try to look for him?' she asked, sitting by Jeronimo's silent form in his place of vigil by the doorway and turning the small revolver over in her hand.

'We still have the Toyota out there.'

The Indian shook his head. 'We must wait.'

And so they waited. When the dark hours were upon them, all Gina had left to hope for was the promise that Perez had made. That he would come back for her.

She couldn't sleep, and didn't even try to. Every movement of the wind, stirring the forest outside the house, brought more wakefulness. She was even afraid to look at her watch, because as the time ticked by, she felt even more scared.

The *maloca* was silent now. The men had returned from the hunt long ago and were asleep with their women on the mats; their children in their hammocks. And as she peered through the darkness toward Jeronimo, she could see that even he was dozing, his head nodding and slumped against his chest. She sighed, praying for morning, as the humid blackness of night surrounded all of them like an uneasy protective cloak.

Gina had no idea how long she lay in that silent disquiet. It could have been hours. But at the touch of a hand on her arm, a scream rose in her throat. The hand came up quickly over her mouth, stifling any sound she tried to make, and as her eyes strained against the darkness, she was suddenly aware of the black shape as it bent over her, forcing her to be still.

His voice came urgent and whispering against her face. 'Don't be scared!' Her eyes stared up, wild and afraid. 'I'm moving my hand away now, but don't make a sound. Do you hear me?'

Gina nodded stiffly, understanding. And as he took his hand away, she gasped for breath. 'Perez!'

'Don't speak! We haven't much time. Listen carefully and do as I say.'

Gina nodded again, able now to recognise his features through the blur. 'Okay. I'm okay,' she whispered back, making a move to rise. 'Are we making a run for it?'

Perez put his hands on her shoulders. 'Yes. But not yet.'

'Not yet? When then?'

'We can't leave tonight.'

'Why?'

'Trust me and listen carefully. We *will* get away, I promise you. But first, you must give me some time.'

'How can I do that?'

'Tomorrow, when the village is awake, you must act as though you believe I'm dead; as though you've accepted the situation.'

'But ...'

'Shh. Don't speak. Just listen. I want you to stay here with Jeronimo and stall for time. He will look out for you. He knows the situation.'

She glanced over to where the Indian had been sleeping a little while ago to find him wide awake, standing with Malakiyaua, watching Perez and herself at the other side of the house.

She turned back to Perez, feeling his small shake of her shoulders as he went on, 'Jeronimo has already been briefed, remember?' When she nodded, he continued again, his whispered voice becoming even more urgent now. 'At eleven o'clock, make some excuse and come to the river, to the place where Luis got hurt.' She nodded again. 'Caninde and I will be waiting. By that time, we'll have a boat standing by.'

'Perez!' She caught at his arm. 'Did you find Elena?'

'No.' Gina paused, not wanting to ask, but knowing she had no choice. 'Perez? Did you kill Lapotikee?'

'Yes.'

'But why?'

His reply was brief and to the point. 'It was either him or me.' She saw the grim lines deepen his mouth. 'I'll explain all these things some other time. What is more important now is that these next few hours will be dangerous; I don't have to spell it out.' He paused for a moment. 'Look, I hate leaving you alone again like this, but I have to. I have no choice if we're to get safely away.'

'But why can't we make a dash for it now?'

He sounded impatient. 'Because we haven't got a boat yet!'

'Can't we use the Toyota?'

He shook his head. 'No. It's guarded. Both trucks are. Besides, we won't be able to get out of here by land, we have to take the river.' His eyes softened a little at her alarmed gaze, and he added reassuringly, 'Don't worry, we'll make it. It's just that we need more time; and by staying here, you'll give it to us.

'They think I'm dead, and I want them to keep thinking that for the next few hours. If they believed for one minute that either of us was alive,' he nodded his head to where Caninde waited outside the house, 'they would hunt us down like dogs. Believe me, I know what I'm doing. You must trust me.'

'I do.' She managed a small smile. 'And don't worry, I always do as I'm told.'

'I'll bet!' He smiled briefly, holding her to him for a moment. 'Remember, eleven o'clock!'

'I'll be there.'

'Eleven,' he repeated. Then he was gone as silently as he had come.

When daylight came, Gina got up and went into the House of Strangers to change her clothes. She glanced at her watch. It was already after 8.00, and the village was awake. She went over to Elena's hammock, nausea souring her stomach as she thought of what the girl must have gone though.

Her eyes drifted to Sinon's empty hammock. How she despised the Greek! But now she knew he'd been lying to her the day before. Perez was alive! She pulled herself together, determined to act out the little game and play her part of grieving lover. It was vital, because their lives depended on it.

She collected some of her things together and packed them into her case. Her camera came next. There would be no time now for photography! And she stowed it away with the rest. Afterwards, she went outside and strolled casually toward the Toyota, the ever-present Jeronimo by her side. She recognised the guard. He was the one she'd seen with the mule.

Gina smiled at him as she opened up the back and placed

her case inside, hoping she looked suitably subdued, which was a sentiment she was far from feeling! This hadn't turned out to be the happiest trip of her life!

A moment of panic swept over her as she crossed back to the House of Strangers. Out of the corner of her eye she saw Sinon standing with Santana by the chief's house, and she could feel their eyes on her, watching every movement, as she walked coolly on.

'Gina! Have you eaten yet?' called Sinon.

'No.'

'Have you no appetite this morning?'

She paused, looking stone-faced back at the Greek. 'I'll have something later.'

'Come, come, little one. You must eat. We have a long journey ahead, and you will need your strength.'

'I'm not hungry.'

'Ah, yes, I understand. Grieving takes one's appetite away.'

Gina gave a deep sigh, answering calmly. 'Yes, I suppose it does.'

She prayed she looked convincing. She walked slowly on toward the house, quelling the powerful urge to run. She must keep a level head. She could feel Sinon's eyes still upon her, and she pretended to wipe away a tear, walking on slowly, her steps measured.

Later, sitting cross-legged with the women at their work, she gave a surreptitious glance at her watch. Ten-thirty! Half an hour to go! She looked over to the Toyota. Less than fifty yards away from her, Sinon and a couple of the Indians were already preparing to leave. They were securing the sacks of pelts with ropes. Gina shivered suddenly. Sinon had ordered Elena killed last night. And perhaps Perez! How many more would have to die because of him, before they were safely out of the Xingu?

Near the appointed time, she got to her feet, her hand closing over the revolver. Jeronimo moved away, giving her the signal. He headed silently toward the river, and Gina looked back at Sinon. The muscles of her stomach were already tight, and the adrenaline flowed. She felt a little like a condemned prisoner making a bid for escape.

Sinon glanced across expressionlessly, and she smiled at him. Thankfully, he seemed not to have noticed Jeronimo's departure, and with an air of indifference, Gina strolled toward the House of Strangers, turning her back on the river.

It was the longest distance she had ever walked. Quite openly, she skirted around the back of the house, knowing that Sinon was still keeping his eye on her. Once out of his sight, she dodged swiftly behind the trees, hoping his curiosity would be allayed by his belief that she was merely answering a call of nature. She looked back again, but Sinon was now on the truck examining the pelts. Gina smiled, her hopes lifting as she fled along the path that led to the river.

Unnoticed, she managed to reach the river bank. Then, satisfied that she had not been followed, she looked desperately one way and the other for a glimpse of Perez.

'This way, Gina!'

'Perez! Where are you?'

'Here! This way!'

She turned quickly in the direction of the voice. The black bow of a canoe nosed its way along the bank, pushing through the tangle of undergrowth beneath her. And as she made her way toward it, she recognised the blurred faces of Caninde and Jeronimo. Reaching the water's edge, she jumped down into the boat, feeling Perez's arm reach out to steady her and break her fall. And then they were off, with Perez pushing the canoe away from the bank.

Within minutes, they were free from the tangled roots of the mangrove swamp and out into the smooth river, moving swiftly with the current and away from Sinon Demetrios – out toward the country of the Waura.

At first the river flowed like a silk ribbon, but it soon changed its mood. After a little less than half an hour it became a torrent, racing toward the Amazon and swollen by the rains. Gina took a paddle from Perez, and the four of them battled against the upriver current. Then Caninde held up his hand. 'Perez! They're coming!'

Perez turned back to look. Gina, too. Behind them, like specks on the water, three boats were already in pursuit.

'It didn't take them long!' Perez muttered.

'What do we do?' Gina asked. 'Make for the bank?'

'No. Caninde! Keep going!' He glanced at Gina, ordering, 'Keep your head low if they come any nearer. It could get rough.'

With only two men to a canoe, their pursuers' lesser weight made it easier for them to bear down on them. Six against four. Reasonable odds. But then there was the crack of rifle fire, and instinctively they crouched low. Perez ordered Gina and the two Indians to paddle harder, as he reached down for his gun. Gina glanced quickly at the small collection of arms in the bottom of the boat.

'Is it Sinon?'

'Can't be anyone else.' Perez gave an indeterminate grunt, checking his aim. The other canoes were right behind, less than a few hundred yards away. He looked around at the river. It had broadened out now, where the smaller tributaries merged. 'He'll have another go, I think, before we reach Waura country.'

'How far from the Waura are we?'

'About fifteen minutes.'

'Then I'd better give you a hand.' Gina threw down the paddle and grabbed a rifle, propping it on her shoulder and taking aim.

Perez glanced down. 'You haven't a clue – I don't recommend it.'

Gina swung to him. '*You* don't recommend it! What else can you suggest? I doubt even you could take on that little lot by yourself!'

He grinned briefly. 'Perhaps not. I'd better load it then.' He took the rifle and jacked a round into the breech before handing it back. 'Good luck, Annie Oakley! It's a good rifle. Just point and hope for the best.'

For a brief second, with the shaft of the rifle pressed up against her cheek, Gina's courage faltered. She looked at Perez nervously. 'I'll do my best.'

'I know you will.'

Perez re-sighted his own rifle and took aim. Soon, the river was echoing to the crackle of rifle fire, and the sudden caterwauling clamour of the startled creatures in the forest around them.

Gina moistened her dry lips, crouching low. She aimed and fired, her arm extended. She almost shut her eyes! Within seconds, a bullet whistled past her ear, splintering the fragile craft. Her heart thudding, Gina fired back, wondering how long they could keep this up; and how long it would be before the canoe was shot from under them and the river swallowed them up.

Keeping their heads down, Caninde and Jeronimo paddled on, maintaining a fair distance between themselves and the hostile rifle fire. By now, Gina had lost track of time. The only thing she knew for certain was that the bullets were far too close for any peace of mind. It all seemed like a dream – or a disaster movie. Then, suddenly, all was quiet. Raising her head warily, Gina looked up. 'What's happened?'

'It's over for now.' Perez took the rifle from Gina's shaking hand and picked up the paddle again. 'Nice work. I don't think you hit anything, but at least you scared 'em. Look!' He pointed downriver. 'We're losing them!'

True enough, Gina could see that the Indians were now moving away, and she breathed a sigh of relief. 'But why are they giving up so soon? They could have had us?'

'They daren't risk coming into Waura territory.' He looked back again and smiled grimly. 'They're going away. We're okay now.'

Gina looked downriver, puzzled but glad of the sight of the retreating Indians. There were only four of them now, and one of the boats had vanished. Perhaps her aim hadn't been too bad after all. She turned to Perez, smiling faintly in her relief. 'Thank God that's over. What happens now?'

Perez relaxed, leaning back against the side of the boat and turning his head so that he could look at her straight. 'We'll take a break, I think. We've earned it.' He handed her a water bottle. 'You did okay.'

She drank gratefully. 'Thanks. So did you.'

They paddled on in silence. Around her, as though there was nothing else in the world, the terrible infinity of river and forest went on. No sign of human habitation, just endless shapes of green and grey, rolling endlessly like an ocean as far as the eye could see.

But soon Gina was thinking ahead, and to the new group of Indians waiting further upriver. She looked back at Perez. 'What about the Waura? Are they trouble?'

'Not to me they're not. We're old friends. Anyway, there's a good way to go before we reach their settlement.' He directed the Indians to steer closer to the bank. 'Here, have another drink.' Perez handed her the water bottle again, his eyes red and bleary through lack of sleep.

Some minutes later, they slowed down, paddling nearer to the bank and pushing the canoe on through the shallow reaches.

'*Bloody hell!*' All of a sudden, Perez was thrashing the sullen water with his paddle. 'Piranhas!'

Gina looked down at the swell of water and at the ugly, blue-tinged heads around the canoe.

Perez swore again. 'They're likely after some animal that's trapped in the weeds.'

They pushed on, moving further up the rain-swollen river into the heart of the Waura.

'What happens after this?' Gina asked, weary now and her arms aching.

'We'll spend tonight with the Waura, then we'll strike through the forest to the airstrip.'

'Wasn't there any chance of taking the Toyota?'

'None. You saw the guards Sinon put on it. This boat was the only way.' He frowned, remembering what a fight the Indians had put up. He sat quietly for a moment, then looked at Gina, feeling her eyes move over him in silent assessment. He pointed across to the tall mass of trees growing thickly along the banks. 'Won't be long now.'

'Good.'

'It's hard to believe that, from here, those trees cover only about seven miles before they thin out into white sandy country. Another half an hour and we'll be out of the Xingu.'

Colin Matheson sat uneasily in his leather chair and read the letter for the third time. Couldn't Gina talk about anything but Perez?

His eyes drifted to the photograph on his desk, and he picked it up. His wife's eyes smiled back at him from the silver frame, her arm gently curved around the pretty, pig-tailed child that was their daughter.

He shook his head, putting it back. Would Carol have approved of Perez? He knew nothing of the man. Nobody did! Was he right for Gina? Matheson doubted it. But then, what man would ever be good enough for Gina? He smiled a little, thinking perhaps he was just being a father!

He looked up as Mark Baxter came into his office.

'Is that from Gina?' the boss's son asked.

'Yes. It came two days ago.'

'Is everything okay?'

Matheson leaned forward in his chair, no longer smiling. He resented the interruption, and turned back to the pile of papers waiting for his attention. 'Shouldn't it be?'

'Does she say anything about the accident?'

Matheson's head jerked up again. 'What accident?'

Baxter perched himself on the edge of the desk. 'The accident to the kid. Some Indian kid who was with Gina and Perez. He fell into the river and was almost half-killed. He's in the hospital now. The plane brought him from Cachimbo.'

'What the hell happened?'

Baxter looked at his watch. 'I don't know. The kid's too ill to say much yet – just babbles. All we've managed to get out of him is that he was with Perez and Gina.' He picked up a metal paperweight and tossed it around in his hand. 'I'm worried, Colin. Perez is supposed to be looking after Gina, and I don't trust the guy.'

'Apparently, Gina does,' Matheson replied quietly. 'Her letter is full of him. He seems to have made quite an impression, and I respect her judgement.'

'I know him better than Gina.'

'I expect you do,' answered Matheson dryly. 'I know there's no love lost between you two. But Weber spoke well enough of him.'

'Weber doesn't know him!' Baxter sounded tense. 'Anyway, I'm going down to Cachimbo to see what's up.'

Colin was silent, his face turned toward the window. Then, abruptly, he stood up, pushing his chair away. 'Do you really believe there's trouble up there?'

'Yes, I do. And I'm certain Perez is involved.'

'In that case, I'm coming with you. Gina's my daughter, and if she's in any danger, I want to be there.'

'Two Dutchmen have booked the plane for this afternoon. I'm cadging a lift.'

'Cadge one for me too. And while you're at it, make sure Fred Armstrong knows we're coming. If your instincts are right, and there is some trouble, we may have to go out as far as the highway airstrip!

13

The trees thinned out as Perez's small party approached the village. Five tall, thatched-roofed dwellings bordered the river's bank; the only accommodation in the commune to shelter its hundred or so inhabitants, so Perez explained. And a dozen or so naked, brown-skinned men were already ranging along the bank, curious at the prospect of the canoe's arrival.

'The Waura?' Gina leaned forward to get a better look, a tinge of apprehension edging into her tone at the sight of the formidable-looking bows, arrows and machetes in the Indians' hands.

'Yes,' came Perez's dry retort. 'Do they scare you?'

'A little.'

'Don't worry. They won't harm us. Their chief is an old friend of mine.'

Minutes later, four tired, insect-plagued travellers pulled into the bank to be greeted by a strong, stocky man. He was Aritana, the Waura chief, and hearing long since of their impending arrival, he bade them welcome, embracing Perez warmly before leading them into his village.

Chatting easily in dialect, Perez and the chief exchanged news as they walked toward the five houses, giving Gina the opportunity to look around. These Waura Indians, like the ones at Santana's village, wore no clothes. But, with their painted faces, they were more handsome. Their features were cultured, and they were taller, too. Strips of red cloth bound their arms, and their fine-cut lips broke more easily into a friendly smile.

When the chief finally left them, allowing them to settle in, Perez told her more about the Wauras' way of life. He showed her the mask house and the flute house and, along the river's bank, the sculptured birds that adorned the shore. These original, primitive carvings were magnificent, and Gina soon became absorbed in watching a boy of nine or ten smooth the mud feathers of an egret into shape. It amazed her that such beauty could be carved from nothing but the skeletal shape of a few broken branches.

Further along, she stopped again to watch another boy as he moulded a lump of sticky red clay into the perfect lines of a heron. He grinned eagerly at them when it was finished, placing it by the water's edge to dry and turning it so that it looked out onto the water. Even without its plumage, the clay heron seemed alive; poised and waiting for an imaginary fish.

'These carvings are superb,' Gina murmured, looking back to Perez.

'Yes, they are,' he agreed, enjoying her delight at the Indians' art. 'Perhaps we can have one for a wedding present.'

Gina glanced at him sharply in case he was joking, but his face was serious!

Perez went on, 'And, look here.' He moved closer to one of the houses. 'The women aren't short on talent either.'

'Did they make these?' Great round bowls and dishes lay everywhere, unglazed yet perfectly thrown.

'Yes. As you can see, they have a flair for ceramics.' He circled his hand, and Gina was impressed by the evidence of the Indian women's craft. She shook her head, silently acknowledging the money they would fetch if they were on sale back home.

'Sometimes, though,' Perez told her more quietly as they walked on around the clearing, 'their ingenuity can stir up quite a bit of trouble. It's not unheard of for the village to be raided by other, less talented Indians. They often take the Waura women away.'

'Don't they have women of their own?'

'Yes, but not like the Waura. These women are prized. The

other tribes are jealous of the Waura men because of their clever, pottery-making wives, so they steal them. As a matter of fact, Aritana was telling me that some of his men have just got back from searching for some of the women.'

'Is that why they look so ferocious?'

'Could be, and I can't say I blame them.'

'Why, what happened?'

'It seems that a couple of the women and their children were taken by some of the Tskikao a couple of nights ago. They're a pretty wild bunch, and the Waura went half across the savannah until they found their people again and brought them back.' He threw Gina a wry, sideways glance. 'Justice is swift here. Chief Aritana has no time for abductors; he orders them killed on sight.'

Gina pulled a rueful face. 'That's swift all right.'

They moved on. The five houses made up the entire village, and one had been put at their disposal. And when they went into it, Gina was glad to see that water to wash in had been placed by the door.

Later on, when they'd bathed as best they could in the cold, brackish water and had eaten their meal of turtle eggs and fruit, they were finally alone. Holding Perez's hand briefly, Gina was only too aware of the tension in him. By the look of him, the hard trek, the long night watches, the scuffle with Santana's men and the death of Lapotikee were beginning to take their toll. Sensing his weariness, her thoughts began to drift toward the things they might have to face in the morning. 'How far to the airstrip now?'

'Two days.'

She frowned. 'As long as that?'

'We should reach the highway the day after tomorrow, then we'll make for Fred and Sheila's place.'

'And before that? Tomorrow night, for instance? Do we camp?'

''Fraid so. They haven't got around to building hotels in the forest yet.' He turned to look at her, his face almost grey in the fading light and etched with a cynicism she had come to recognise. 'Your trip hasn't turned out exactly how you imagined, has it?'

Gina shrugged. 'I'm not complaining.'

He sprawled himself down onto the mat, stretching his aching limbs and making room for her as she came to sit beside him.

He turned to watch her as she tried to make herself comfortable on the hard earth floor, wondering what she was really making of all the things that had happened. She hadn't complained, but how different she looked now from the fresh, smiling girl he'd first met at Cachimbo.

She was still smiling, but her red shirt and khaki slacks were faded now, dark patches of sweat staining the armpits; and in spite of her recent bath, her grime-caked face was still streaked with lines of perspiration. Perez turned away. He wondered morosely if she regretted her trip; if she still trusted his judgement after what had happened to Elena. 'Look, I'm sorry I've got you into this mess. It wasn't intended.'

Her stomach clenched. 'I know that. Forget it.'

'You can't say it's been a success.'

'Oh, I don't know. I've learned a lot, and I've certainly seen more than I bargained for. I've lived with the Indians, eaten fried cicadas and almost been shot out of the river.' She threw him a brief smile. 'What more could a girl ask for? And, on top of all that, I've managed to get some terrific photographs for my book, if I ever manage to get hold of my camera again. I think I can safely say that it's been quite an experience.'

Perez nodded his head. 'I suppose you could say that.' He lay down, flattening his aching back against the straw mat and looking up through the gap in the roof at the flaring red of the dying sun. He was tired. Bone-weary tired. His lined eyes drifted back to the girl beside him, just visible now in the darkness. He wished he had the strength left to make love to her, but he hadn't. There was a long silence, and when he spoke again, his words were a little slurred with the effort. 'And where do I figure in this experience of yours?'

Gina looked down. 'You, Perez?' She laughed softly. 'You *are* the experience.'

He didn't answer, and she bent over to kiss him. But whether he'd heard her reply or not, she couldn't say. Perez was already fast asleep.

The next morning, after they'd eaten their breakfast of piquia, the succulent yellow fruit that the Indians loved so well, they set off again, this time on foot. Aritana's men loaded them up with supplies, and with Perez and Caninde leading and Jeronimo at her back, Gina tramped along the narrow winding track that was to lead them to the highway.

They walked for a long time without speaking; no-one saying a word, each one conserving their strength for the long haul ahead. The silence was complete, except for the sound of Jeronimo's uneven breathing behind Gina. Now and then, sporadic showers of rain drenched them, making her swear inwardly. She should be used to the rain by now, but she wasn't. Soon her clothes were drenched and her feet soaked, and now, as the undergrowth grew more dense, she could hardly see a thing.

They walked without a break for over three hours, not even the brilliance of the waxy red flowers around her lightening Gina's mood. Eventually, the effort of putting one foot in front of the other was becoming an ordeal. The fragrance of the orchids drifted down from high above, and dark, damp clumps of leaves brushed against her skin, scratching and painful.

Gina lost count of how often she stumbled as the slimy track sucked relentlessly at her boots. And she had no idea of time. Now and then, Perez looked back to see if she was all right. 'Are you okay?'

'I'm fine.' She forced a smile, but her face gave her away.

When the light began to fade, they made camp. In a clearing, the Indians lit a fire. Their hasty departure up the Xingu had made it impossible for them to tote any equipment, and Caninde and Jeronimo set about making beds for the night out of the forest's scattered leaves and twigs. One for themselves and one for Perez and Gina.

They ate piquia again. It was a quick supper, none of them saying very much. Afterwards, Perez and Caninde moved about quietly, setting warning traps around the clearing.

'Expecting trouble?' Gina asked, making herself comfortable on the bed of leaves and feeling a little like a Babe in the Wood.

Perez turned, grim-faced, and answered flatly, 'This is Txukahamei country. They're not so friendly as the Waura. I'm making sure, that's all. Just a temporary survival system.'

When he was finished, he came to lie beside her, the last of the firelight flickering and dying and a small humid breeze blowing up from the west. They turned to face each other and savoured a wonderful kiss.

Soon, contrary to all her expectations, Gina fell asleep, worn out by the physical exertion of the day, and glad of the comforting arm of Perez as he draped it loosely across her shoulders. Some time in the night, she felt his kiss brush her face again and shivered in her sleep. She woke up properly only once, and it was not from a likely attack by the Txukahamei, but from yet another brief, torrential downpour.

At first light they set off again, following the same compass direction. They were climbing steeply now, and by mid-afternoon, exhausted and feeling as though balls of lead had been tied to her feet, Gina emerged at last into daylight. Now, the jungle was behind them. Relieved, she stood still on the plateau, delighting in the sun's warmth and letting the sweeter air embrace her skin.

Perez walked to the edge, gesturing with his left hand. 'Look! Come and see!'

Coming back to earth, Gina went to stand beside him, catching her breath at the long golden snake of road that lay before them. 'The highway!' She said it softly, tight-lipped, her blue eyes gazing down with an unbelieving stare. 'Thank God!'

Perez looked at her slowly. 'It's not over yet. You realise that, don't you?'

She looked up with a quick twist of her head. 'You mean Sinon?'

He nodded. 'He's not going to give up easily. We know too much.'

'Do you think he'll be at the airstrip?'

He shrugged. 'I daresay. I know for a fact that he's expecting someone, and the plane's due either tonight or first thing tomorrow; but I doubt they'll try to land at night.'

'I wonder if Dad got my letter?' she murmured, noticing smoke in the distance. It was probably her dad's firm, burning up more of the forest!

Perez had seen the plumes of smoke too. And he must have sensed her thoughts, because his response came back quickly, edged with derision. 'Your dad is a top dog at Baxter-Weber! The guys at Cachimbo probably made sure the mail was delivered even before getting Luis into hospital. The company is always given first priority.'

She glanced up at him. 'You sound bitter.'

'I've every reason to be bitter! The company makes me sick. Even seeing the highway turns my stomach. If the company didn't build the roads, the forest would be left in peace. And it's all for the profit of a few!'

'You work for the company, too,' she reminded him briskly.

'I work for myself! The money I earn goes to protect the forest, not to destroy it.'

'I'm not condoning what Baxter-Weber have done. But you have to admit, the highway's quite a feat of engineering.'

He looked at her obliquely, deep sarcasm glittering in the dark eyes. 'And, being the surveyor's daughter, you know all about engineering!'

'For God's sake, Perez! Why are you angry with me? You know what I think!' Her question was loaded with contempt. 'After all, you can't stop progress singlehanded! Oh, I know the company's into other things now besides rubber, but the big ranchers are taking their share, too. And it's not my fault, or Dad's either for that matter, that the big boys are clearing parts of the forest.'

'Oh, spare me the helplessness, Gina. Whose fault is it then? Who makes the most profit out of it all?'

'You're just as much to blame!' she came back impatiently. 'How much did you charge the company to bring me here? And, something else ...' She took a deep angry breath. 'If you're such a saint, why do you have anything to do with a man like Sinon? You knew what his game was! Why *did* you?'

Perez hadn't time to argue. 'Okay, point taken,' he interrupted harshly. 'I suppose we're all to blame. But it's all this damage that's being done that gets to me!'

He wrinkled his eyes, gazing into the distance at the smoke-blackened sky. 'An acre a minute!' he gritted through his teeth. He turned back to her briskly. 'At least by taking people through, I can show them what their kids, or their kid's kids, will be deprived of a hundred years from now.'

She glared at him. 'And in the meantime we've *all* to suffer the blame! You seem to have forgotten that there are just as many people doing their best to save it!'

'That's enough!' He grasped her arm, leading her away from the plateau. 'We'll talk about this later. Let's see what kind of a reception is waiting for us at the airstrip.' A moment later, he turned to her and grinned. 'Was that our first row?'

'Probably the first of many,' she said, still smarting. At that moment, Gina could see another Perez from the man who had made love to her. But in her heart she knew he was right. Which made her love him even more.

The going was easier now. They moved south toward the commercial face of the highway. The track widened, and soon, in the distance, Gina began to pick up the indistinct sounds of bulldozers.

Perez stopped, hitching his pack more comfortably onto his shoulders and looking back to her. 'Come on, not long now. Let's hope we've made it before Sinon. How are you feeling?' His eyes were sympathetic, so different from how they flashed when he was roused.

'I'm tired,' she answered, 'but I'll survive.' He grinned, putting a hand up and brushing back her hair. She loved those little gestures. She looked up at him. 'What happens when we get to Fred's? Apart from flying out, I mean.'

'I'll have to radio Belem. The gun-running has to be stopped. And quick!'

'I agree.'

'The police will be interested in the cocaine, too. They'll need to find out just where it's going and who to!' He frowned distractedly. 'I only wish I could get my hands on those damned papers that Elena had. Those would put paid to Sinon once and for all.'

'Do you think Sinon has them?'

'No, I don't. If he had, he wouldn't want to shut us up so fast. There'd be no proof against him. I think he believes we're carrying them.' He started off again. 'Come on. I'm sorry I'm pushing you, but we need to get to the airstrip fast.'

They walked swiftly on, reaching the highway in under an hour. As they stepped onto the hard surface, Perez stretched out a warning arm and brought them to a halt. 'Listen,' he muttered. 'Can you hear that?'

They listened, straining their ears, and soon Gina heard it too. The sound of an engine growing ever nearer. 'Do you think it might be Sinon?'

'Who knows? Although it doesn't sound like the Toyota to me. Come on, this way.'

They set off again, stepping off the hard grit of the highway's surface and keeping out of sight in the brush. The forest was giving way to scrubby fields, and by the look of the new-planted softwood trees all around, someone was already making an attempt to heal the forest's wounds. The noise of the engine became more distinct. It wasn't a bulldozer or a truck, just the spluttering friendliness of a tractor.

Perez increased his pace. 'It's Fred! We've made it!'

Gina stumbled on behind him, switching her eyes to the tractor as it rumbled into sight. As soon as he saw them, Fred Armstrong gave a pleased yell, turning the vehicle and driving toward them at full speed. And, as she clambered aboard, Gina felt she had never been so glad to see anyone in all of her life.

For the first time in weeks, Gina stretched out on a comfortable bed. She had slept deeply and for a long time. Opening her eyes, she wondered for a moment where she was; then, looking through the mosquito net into the hazy light, she remembered. She was in Fred and Sheila's bed at the airstrip.

Earlier, she had bathed, and Sheila had left a change of clothes for her folded over a chair. Gina got up and put them on, turning as she heard the light tap on the door.

'Come in. I'm up and decent.'

It was Perez. When she saw him, she wished she wasn't. He looked great; rested and alert. Noticing the oversized mannish outfit she had on, he grinned. 'At least you can get into Sheila's gear! I had to pass on Fred's pants and shirt.'

'You look better.'

'I feel better!' he told her cheerfully. 'I've slept like a log, and Sheila washed my things. I don't smell so much like a hog now.'

Gina smiled. She was remembering the scent of his body, and no hog could ever make her react the way she did to him. 'Did you get manage to through to Belem?'

He nodded. 'Yes.'

'And?'

He pulled up a cane chair and sat straddled across it, his arms resting along the back. 'They're on their way.'

'Who are? The police?'

He nodded again, apparently finding the sight of her loosely-covered body of more interest than the authorities. 'Mmm ...' He glanced up, thrusting distracting thoughts out of his mind. 'And the army, too, by the sound of it.'

'The army?'

'The lot. They won't waste any time where gun-running is concerned. Santana will wonder what's hit him.'

'What will they do to him?'

He shrugged. 'If they can prove anything, he'll be sent for

trial.' His eyes were strafing her body, and she felt very hot in spite of the fan in the ceiling.

'If not, at least it'll put him off for a while. Trouble is, it's their word, Santana's and Sinon's, against mine. And they'll have covered their tracks pretty well.' His face darkened with growing frustration. 'I just wish I could get my hands on those papers.'

Gina was silent, thinking of the village and of the good people in it, whose lives would be devastated soon by the greed of Santana and his men.

She was thinking, too, of her belongings still in Sinon's truck; not only her clothes, which didn't matter, but her beloved camera. So much for her book! How could she hope to do her bit for the forest now, without her hard-earned pictorial proof?

'I feel partly to blame, somehow,' she murmured.

He looked up, surprised. 'Why? What have you to blame yourself for?'

Gina shook her head doubtfully. 'If I hadn't decided to come on this damned trip, Sinon would still be in Belem and Elena would still be alive.'

She held Perez's gaze, seeing the look of compassion come into his eyes. He smiled bleakly, saying quietly, 'That's a crazy thing to say. None of this is any of your fault. It would have happened sooner or later. I would have come back to the forests with Sinon anyway, and I would have had to face the day of reckoning with him before much longer.' He turned away from her for a moment, but not before Gina had seen the unmistakable glimmer of pain in his eyes. 'And as for Elena ...' He sighed deeply. 'She knew she was cutting a fine line, but it was a lousy way to die all the same.'

'Yes.'

'Anyway ...' he stood up briskly, swinging his legs from around the chair. 'Let's ...' He moved toward her, a quizzical smile on his face, but he got no further. Suddenly the door burst open and Fred Armstrong's head appeared. 'Perez! We've got company! Looks like Sinon!'

Gina couldn't feel disappointed that the moment had broken. It was the news they'd been waiting for.

Perez swung round, moving very fast, and the next thing Gina knew, she was following him out of the room and to the windows at the front of the house.

Her heart sank when she saw the dust trails of two trucks, coming at speed, and even more so as she recognised the Toyota, knowing it was likely to be Sinon at the wheel, with Santana sitting beside him in the passenger seat.

Colin Matheson wasn't taking much notice of what was going on around him in the plane. He was thinking of Gina and whether or not she was safe.

Glancing sideways at the pale face of the man sitting beside him, he wondered vaguely whether Gina would be as pleased to see Mark Baxter as the man believed she would. He doubted it. According to her letter, Perez seemed to be the only thing that pleased his daughter these days.

He looked across at the plane's other two passengers. Normally a gregarious man, Colin had made an attempt at conversation, but hadn't managed to get a word out of either of them. He knew they were Dutch, so perhaps language was a barrier, but they hadn't spoken a word to each other either.

He turned to look out of the porthole. It wouldn't be long before they reached the airstrip now and, with his precise surveyor's mind, he was already going over his arrangements once again. If the supplies hadn't yet arrived, he was prepared to stay with Fred and Sheila Armstrong. Vaguely, he heard the nasal crackle of the plane's radio. He glanced across to watch the pilot as he adjusted the earphones.

'Repeat! Please repeat! Over!'

The crackling garbled message was repeated as instructed, and, hearing it, the pilot gave a low whistle. 'Got it! Message received and understood! Over!'

He turned to look at his passengers, his voice strangely tense over the low drone of the engines. 'It seems there's a spot of trouble at the strip,' he told them. 'I've been given instructions to turn back.'

'Trouble? What trouble?' shouted Colin. Could it be anything to do with Gina?

'Fred didn't say. Only that we get the hell out of here and radio for help.'

'But ...' Colin half rose from his seat '... but suppose it's my daughter, we ...'

Baxter turned quickly to Colin, looking nervous. 'Why should it be Gina? No, Colin, it's probably the Indians or the squatters again. We'd better do as Fred says. If there's trouble, let's get out of here and send more help ...'

He broke off abruptly at the sudden movement from the Dutchmen. For no accountable reason, the quiet, rather bored atmosphere of the plane had changed to one charged with danger. Then the strangers were on their feet, and with a quick menacing movement, the older one had reached the pilot's seat! He was pointing a gun at the man's head and glaring at them too!

'What the hell are you doing?' Baxter was clearly scared, as his voice was shaking. Colin was too shocked to speak! What was going on?

'Quiet!' ordered the younger man, who had been standing next to Matheson. 'Don't move. Either of you!' With slow, deliberate movements, he backed up the narrow aisle, gun in hand, to join his companion by the pilot. 'Not a muscle!'

Colin glanced swiftly at the pilot, watching tensely as he saw his hand make a furtive attempt to reach for the radio switch. But the Dutchman saw him too and pressed the gun harder into his neck. 'Don't try to be clever,' he said quietly. The pilot's mouth had sagged slightly open, and an expression of stunned surprise was etched across his face. He looked up at the Dutchman, his grey eyes bleak. 'No use trying to get rid of me,' he said. 'Who else'll keep this thing in the air?'

'We know that.' The Dutchman signalled with a nod of his head to his companion, who then moved back as far as Colin and pressed the cold muzzle of his gun into his neck. He stared down and caught hold of Colin's tie, twisting it like a tourniquet. 'But there's nothing to stop us getting rid of this one.'

'You'll never get away with this!'

'No?' The stocky Dutchman smiled. 'Just watch us, pilot. For your passengers' safety, do as you're told and fly on to the strip.'

'And then what?'

'We land. What else? We have our business to complete.'

'What the hell?' Colin struggled. He was almost half out of his seat, but the Dutchman pushed him back. The man's hold on him was painful, but it meant very little to him now. He tried to twist away, sweat springing out from every pore.

'All of you, be quiet,' the first man warned. 'If you do as we say, you won't get hurt. We land and you'll get out!' He waved the gun around in the air. 'After we've disposed of you, we'll refuel.' He smiled coldly at the pilot. 'And when we have picked up our business associates, you can fly us on to Medellin!'

'*Medellin?*' Realisation suddenly dawned on the pilot. 'Medellin?' he repeated. 'Colombia?'

'How quickly you understand,' the Dutchman said softly.

14

Everyone inside the building stared as the Toyota and the accompanying vehicle screeched to a stop in a cloud of dust at the far side of the airstrip. Immediately after, the ominous silence was broken by the fractured crackle of the airstrip radio.

'Redbird calling Airstrip Five! Airstrip Five, over! Are you receiving me? Redbird requesting permission to land! Over!'

Fred Armstrong glanced at Perez uncertainly. 'They're coming in, damn it!' No-one else in the room moved as Fred stared at Perez. 'They must be mad! I've warned them!'

Perez said nothing for a moment, staring impassively at the sky. Then he said grimly, 'Better bring them in.'

'You realise what you're saying?' Fred kept his voice low.

'Can't be helped, we'll have to risk it.' Perez had clearly given the situation thought. 'They could be running short of fuel by now.'

'Right. Pity the chopper's still at Cachimbo, though. We could have got you out.'

Fred slipped quickly across the room to sit down at the table. He switched on the radio, speaking into the mouthpiece with an aggressive urgency. 'Calling Redbird! Airstrip Five receiving you. Make your landing from the south. Repeat. Make your landing from the south. Over!'

'Message understood! Approaching Airstrip Five from the south. Four passengers aboard. ETA fifteen minutes. Redbird out!'

Fred put down the mouthpiece and glanced down at the open notebook on his desk before looking back to Perez. 'Four passengers. That'll be Matheson, Baxter and the two Dutch businessmen.'

Perez felt Gina's hand catch hold of his sleeve as she looked across at Fred. 'Did you say Colin Matheson?' he asked. 'And Mark Baxter?'

'That's right. And two other guys.'

Perez turned to look at Gina, smiling grimly. 'Looks like they're sending in the cavalry.'

'But what the hell is Dad doing coming all the way out here – and Mark as well?'

'Perhaps they think I can't get you home without their help. They don't exactly look on me as Tarzan, do they?'

'But it seems such a waste of time. It doesn't make sense!'

Sheila Armstrong looked up from her sewing, putting it aside and commenting dryly, 'Nothing seems to make sense these days.' She stood up and moved to the door. 'Gina, how about helping me make some coffee? It looks like we're all going to need it.'

Gina nodded, looking at Perez now with a wry expression on her face. 'Well, Tarzan, do you want some? Shall I help Sheila with the coffee?'

'Might as well.'

'Will you be able to manage without me?'

'I'll try.'

When the two women had left the room, Fred rose from the table and went to stand at the window beside Perez. 'Quite a girl.'

'Yes, she is.'

'Now what?'

'We wait.'

'Right.'

The minutes dragged by as the two men stood together by the fly-screened windows looking out onto the far side of the runway, where the Toyota and the truck had pulled in. Perez made a quick estimate of the number of Indians in the second truck; at least a dozen, maybe more.

Fred lit a cigarette. 'Are you going to tell me what's going on? What the hell is Sinon playing at? What's he doing just sitting by the runway like some bloody sphinx?'

'He's making sure we don't get on the plane.'

'But why, for Christ's sake? Surely, he knows you're both in here with us? What's his game?'

Perez gave an expressive shrug. 'Sinon needs the plane even more than we do. I doubt he'll make his move before it lands. If my guesses are right, his contacts are on that plane; and without them, his whole deal goes down. He'll be saving us for extra insurance – especially me. He thinks I have Elena's papers.'

'What papers?'

Perez moved across to the table. He filled a glass with water and took a sip, then said quietly, 'Sinon's in deep. I have no proof, but apart from the fur trade, which we all know about, it looks like he's into drugs now.'

'Drugs?'

Perez nodded. 'Yes. And when you think about it, it's not a bad scheme. Knowing Sinon, he's probably got a few distributors along the river, and it would be easy to use the normal trade routes. It's not bad thinking, especially if you want to keep things quiet from the law. Who'd think of looking here?'

Fred considered. 'I see what you mean. It's about the most isolated part of the world, and it's a tough area to police. But how do you know about the drugs?'

'Elena found them.'

Fred frowned slightly, recalling what Perez had told him about the Greek girl. 'That was unfortunate.'

'Yes, it was. And my theory is that the two guys on the plane ship the stuff from Colombia. The money is exchanged at airstrips like this throughout Brazil. Once the exchange is made, Sinon distributes it through his connections in Manaus and Rio. It's his bank-roll for his arms deals.'

Fred whistled through his teeth. 'If all that's true, then he *is* in pretty deep. But I don't understand it. Why bother with arms, too? There must be more money in narcotics than running a few guns to the Indians. They haven't any money.'

'That's only a side line to keep Santana happy. Sinon needs Santana to control the Indians. He'd never make it alive in the forest or on the river otherwise, and he takes his cut. The real money for arms comes through Venezuela from Nicaragua.'

'How do you know all this?'

'I don't for sure. It's only what I've been able to pick up in the time I've known him. Unfortunately, I still need the proof! And I could have had it with those papers. Elena showed me two documents the night she died. They showed signed deals between Sinon, Santana and the arms dealers. Not only that, there were names in those lists that pointed to where the drugs was coming from, too.'

Fred showed no enthusiasm now. 'Stupid of them to have it all down in black and white; I would have thought Sinon had more sense than that!'

'It was probably Santana's idea. There's no honour among thieves where those two are concerned. And Santana knows that Sinon wouldn't bat an eye about getting rid of him if he could do without him.'

'And Sinon knows you know all that?'

'Yes.' Perez picked up the water again and took another sip.

'Then it's not going to be easy getting you out of here alive.'

Perez shook his head. 'No, but we'll manage.' He turned back to the window to look again at the waiting Toyota. It stood eerily still, clear of the runway, its headlight reflectors glinting dully in the sunlight.

Then Perez's face suddenly stilled, his breath exhaling sharply between his teeth. '*Sonofabitch!*' He stared out at the two trucks.

'Fred!' he ordered urgently. 'Get one of your boys to fetch my two Indians, and as many more as you can find! Some way or another, he's managed to get away from the Toyota without me seeing him!'

In the cool of the tiny kitchen, Gina handed Sheila the tray of coffee, her sense of hopelessness growing. She was praying that the plane carrying her father would land safely. She couldn't bear to lose her dad! Within minutes, she could hear the sound of the plane as it circled the strip. She pulled the fly-screen to one side and looked up at the sky. Moments later, the small silver and red company plane was touching down and taxiing along the strip.

'They're here, Sheila.'

'Right, we'd better get back in there. I don't suppose there'll be time for coffee now.'

'Okay.' Gina's voice was nervous and uneasy. She glanced outside again before pulling down the screen. The dust from the plane was obliterating most of the runway. But then, as the red dust cloud cleared, she froze, letting a small cry escape her. Santana's Indians came into focus. Within minutes, the runway was crawling with them, and as the plane's door opened, the first face she saw was her father's.

She raced toward the door, with Sheila following behind. But as she pulled it open, she stopped suddenly as she found her way blocked by the broad bulk of Sinon Demetrios. His arm came across the doorway, barring her flight, and his small, piggy eyes fixed coldly on her, waiting. Ten seconds of tense, fearful silence hung over the tiny room like a shroud. Sinon's tone was menacing. 'What's all the hurry, little one?'

Her eyes swung downwards toward his gun. 'Sinon!'

He was smiling now, his round, pale face unshaven. 'Take it easy, English mouse. You're not going anywhere.' He moved his gaze from Gina to Sheila, waving the gun toward her. 'You! Stand back! And no noise from either of you!'

He grasped Gina's arm and twisted it up around her back. She cried out with the sharp pain. Then he beckoned to one of the Indians waiting outside, and Gina struggled even more as the man came in and caught hold of Sheila, forcing her into a painful retreat across the room and tying her up on a chair in the corner. Sinon jabbed the gun against Gina's side. 'Now, little one, it's your turn.'

He pulled on her arm, kicking the door open with his foot and forcing her outside. With his gun trained on the small of her back, he marched her toward the waiting plane.

Keeping his head down, Perez skirted around the back of the house until he was out of sight of Santana's men. He pressed himself flat against the wall as Sinon came out, reining in his impulse to lunge when, with a shock, he saw the man had Gina and was pressing a gun to her back. He swore silently, cursing himself for giving the Greek even a hair's breadth of a chance.

He knew Caninde and Jeronimo would be somewhere close, but he wished he knew precisely where. The squatters' camp wasn't far away, if that was where they'd gone. When they'd asked Perez for a few hours' leave, he'd had no option to but to give it to them. But now he wished he had them beside him. Fred and himself against a dozen of Santana's men was not a pleasant prospect. The odds were firmly in Sinon's favour.

Perez half turned his head to glance quickly to where the plane stood. Santana and his men had encircled the small group of Matheson, Baxter and the pilot, the bait so obvious he almost laughed out loud.

Then he moved cautiously, ducking under the wire strands that separated the house from the strip. He followed the grass border that marked the edge of the runway, making for the tractor and keeping well under cover behind the waiting crates of cargo until he reached the plane.

Crouching low, Perez looked on grimly, fingering his revolver. It wasn't tiny like the one he'd given Gina, but a heavy Magnum. Sinon, with Gina at his front, was standing with his back to Perez now, close to the rear door. Some of the Indians were already loading the pelts into the hold, moving about quickly as Sinon barked out his orders. Perez was within three feet of the Greek. He had him in his sights, but he couldn't risk a shot.

Further away, toward the front of the plane, he could see two Indians holding Gina's father and Baxter at gunpoint. With a gun at his back too, the pilot was stood by the hand-pumps, refuelling the plane from the fifty-gallon drums. A little apart from the rest were the two other passengers, both of them deep in conversation with Santana. They were evidently Sinon's contacts.

For a few tense moments all was quiet, and Perez planned his action. But before he could make a move, all hell seemed to break loose as the sound of someone shooting came from behind. He looked back quickly to see three of Santana's Indians approaching the house, making ready to join the others who had started the attack.

Briefly he caught a glimpse of Fred and Sheila at the window as they fired back. And, to his relief, he saw that Caninde and Jeronimo had arrived to help.

'*Gina!*' Perez jerked his head back at the sound of Matheson's frantic voice. '*Let her go, Sinon!*'

'She's coming to Medellin with me. Your daughter in exchange for two little pieces of paper. A fair bargain, eh?'

With his stomach churning, Perez moved silently round the back of the plane and toward Sinon, stooping low under the plane's belly and using it for cover.

'That's the last of them!' The Greek's voice drifted down to Perez. He sounded confident. His business was almost done, and he felt he was in danger no longer. He had assumed that the conflict going on at the house would be keeping Perez occupied, with no time now to worry about him and his deals. And, as a bonus, he'd got the English girl as his passport. 'Have you got the stuff?' he called to the two Dutchmen.

'Of course, Sinon. Would we have come this far without it?'

'Give it to Santana; he knows what to do.'

'Not until we see the cash!'

'I have the money, don't worry. But I'll keep hold of it until we're on the plane.'

'It is not in the deal that you come back with us. The exchange was to be completed here.'

'The deal has changed. I must accompany you. Things may soon get a little too hot around here for old Sinon. Get back on board before the police find us.'

Sinon signalled to Santana pick up the Dutchmen's cases as the Indians loaded the last of the pelts.

'You!' Sinon addressed the pilot. 'Have you finished?'

'Almost.'

'Then get back in and start her up.'

There wasn't much time left. Perez bent down, lowering his gun and moving forward.

It all seemed to happen in a flash. Sinon was within inches of Perez now, his back toward him and playing right into his hands. Perez moved out of the cover of the plane and edged cautiously toward the Greek. Then, summoning all his energy, he sprang, lunging blindly forward, sending Sinon's gun hand up in the air and smashing the butt of his revolver against the side of his head.

Perez heard the great whoosh of air from the Greek's belly as he folded, white-faced, emitting an unearthly scream. Sinon writhed on the ground, but Perez, looking down, knew he wasn't quite finished yet. He reached out his foot to kick the gun away, but he was a second too late. Instinctively, Sinon rolled over, reaching out. Then. grabbing the gun, he pointed it. A glazed look of stunned surprise was showing in his eyes, but his brain was still ticking over.

In those few volatile seconds, Gina twisted away, her eyes dilated. She wrenched free of Sinon, ramming at him with her foot as she threw herself out of his reach. Suddenly she was running toward her father as he stood by the plane.

Slowly, as if in a trance, the Greek turned on his side, his arm coming up and levelling the gun toward Gina's fleeing back. 'You're not having the bitch either, Perez! You owe me!' His finger tightened around the trigger. 'The girl first, and then you!'

Perez kicked out, hearing the sharp snap of the Greek's wrist as his boot made contact. Sinon let out a scream, but he still held on to the gun and, turning back to Perez, he raised the barrel into his face. Without stopping to think, Perez fired. He might have shot off the whole six bullets, but he didn't stop to count. All he could see now was the pathetic crumpled mass that had once been Sinon. The Greek was dead!

Perez glanced toward the plane. He saw Gina standing by her father, waving her arms and calling out to him. He couldn't hear her. Then, everything was suddenly still. Perez was aware of nothing except the dull thud as the bullet hit him. He spun twice, his body lifting clear off the ground as it fell backwards for at least three feet.

Perez lay staring up into the sun, his face draining of colour until it was almost white. He screwed up his eyes, blinking away the sickening waves of grey dizziness that were starting to wash around him.

The roaring in his ears deafened him and muffled all other sound. He looked up again, this time to catch a glimpse of silver as it flashed above his head. Then great black dragonflies were circling and spinning in his brain.

Perez rolled over as the noise in his ears increased. He heard Gina's voice in the distance, calling his name. He tried to answer, but the words wouldn't come. He was conscious of nothing now. Only blankness as oblivion took over.

15

Colin Matheson looked across at his daughter as her shaking fingers struggled to spoon a speck of dust from the whirling, creamy swirls in the coffee-cup. He was worried about her. God knows, she hadn't been kidding when she'd told him how much she cared for Perez.

Sitting there in the squeaky-clean waiting room of Belem's main hospital, with the aroma of food intermingling with the sharp tang of disinfectant, Colin was dismayed at how distraught his daughter looked.

He thought back again over the last few weeks. Had it all been worth it? Had it been merely self-indulgence? An illusion that Gina might do some good for the forests of Brazil? 'If there hadn't been an improvement, the hospital wouldn't have rung us this morning,' he said, keeping his voice as even as he could.

Gina looked up and smiled at her father. 'Always the optimist, eh, Dad?'

'Well, what else can it be? Perez is out of intensive care. He's been damned lucky!'

'Lucky? So everyone keeps reminding me!' She put the cup down, her fingers trembling. 'Perez almost died saving my life!'

There was a short pause before Colin said quietly, 'I know. He saved all our lives by radioing Belem when he did, thank God.'

Gina shuddered violently as she got to her feet to move restlessly across to the window. She stood silently for a moment looking out. She'd had three weeks of hell! Three weeks of not being able to sleep, eat, or think coherently while she'd waited for Perez to recover his strength.

They had told her more than once that he was improving, but she'd been too afraid to believe it! She knew it was foolish to be so neurotic, as it wouldn't help anything, especially him. But how could she help it when she remembered the violent events of three weeks earlier? When she'd sat by an unconscious Perez in the plane to Belem, being reassured by the doctor that he had been very lucky indeed, because the bullet from Santana's gun had missed his heart by a mere fraction of an inch?

Standing there in the waiting-room, the silence seemed to be closing in on her, and she turned from the window and walked around, her hand gripping even more tightly around the leather bag slung across her shoulder. She had been late that day. The drive from her home to the hospital usually took a little over fifteen minutes. But as she had been sitting beside her father in the car and had looked out at the snarl of traffic along the Avenue Cristoforo, she had known it would take at least an hour.

Her mind drifted again to her lover, who had been lying so desperately ill in his hospital bed. Three weeks earlier, the shooting at the airstrip had hit the national headlines. The whole rotten story of Sinon Demetrios and the Indian, Chief Santana, had broken out in a roar of public outrage. As Perez had lain bleeding to death on the red earth of the airstrip, the place had been suddenly surrounded. It had been impossible for the Indians to escape. They had tried to run, scattering back into the forest like fleas on a dog, but armed policemen and the military had flushed them out, and their panic-stricken attempts to break loose had been cut off finally.

Santana was finished, as were the Dutchmen. They hadn't stood a chance of getting away. It had taken less than an hour for the police to round up the chief's small army of followers. They had been disarmed and bundled into the waiting helicopters to be despatched to Belem, and now the Indian was awaiting trial for the attempted murder of Perez.

Gina bit her lip, remembering. She would never forget seeing Santana's gun aimed at Perez. She had tried to warn him, but he hadn't heard her. And by the time she had reached him, he had ben already on the ground, his lifeblood flowing away. All the way to Cachimbo she had sat with him, holding his hand and frightened out of her wits in case he wouldn't make it.

At Cachimbo, another plane had been waiting to take them to Belem, and for days now he had hovered between life and death, touching consciousness from time to time, not saying a word. Her hand tightened again around her bag. *Oh, Perez,* she cried silently for the thousandth time. *For God's sake, don't let me down now! Please! Please! Come back to me!*

Perez's eyes opened, bright and clear. He looked around the room, taking in the clean-scrubbed walls, the vase of flowers on the locker at his side and the small figure in white who was seated by the window.

He tried to move again but still found it difficult. The nun got up from her chair, moved to his side, and her kindly, intelligent brown eyes flickered over the dials that had been monitoring his vital functions. 'Senhor Perez, welcome back!'

'Who are you?'

'Sister Consuelo. I've been looking after you in hospital.'

Perez blinked, trying to rid the dreams from his skull. 'Where's Gina?' he said.

'Miss Matheson?'

Gina jumped up quickly at the appearance of the white-coated man standing in the doorway. 'Yes?'

'You can see Senhor Perez now, if you will come this way. You too, Mr Matheson.'

They followed the doctor through a labyrinth of corridors until he opened a door of a side ward. 'Senhor Perez has made a remarkable recovery,' he told them. 'He's an exceptionally strong man. Tell him I'll be back to see him in half an hour.'

Colin looked at Gina, then sat down on a small chair outside the room. 'I'll wait here for you, love,' he smiled. 'I'm sure Perez would rather see you than me. Besides, while I'm waiting, there's someone else I'd like to go over and visit.'

Gina nodded, her eyes looking across the room to where the man she loved lay. She was very grateful for her dad's consideration. She just wanted to be alone with Perez!

She moved quietly to stand by his bed. Sister Consuelo, a gentle smile on her face, went out, closing the door behind her.

Gina looked down at Perez, whose eyes were tightly closed. Now, his breathing was even and regular. It was so wonderful to see him off the respirator! A wide strip of bandage was wound across his shoulder where the bullet had been removed. Beneath the bandage, and around the edges, Gina could see the deep bluish marks of bruising, and as she glanced at his face, his hair seemed darker than ever against the stark white of the pillow. Her hand reached out, as though of its own accord, and touched his brow. 'Perez,' she whispered. 'Perez, are you awake?'

He stirred, turning his head. Then, dark eyelashes flickering momentarily, he opened his eyes. 'Gina?'

'How are you feeling, darling?'

'A bit groggy, but I'm told I'll live.' It was an effort to speak. 'You've had me worried sick.'

'Have I?' He reached for her hand. 'Sorry. I didn't mean to.'

She smiled. 'Don't be silly. I'm just grateful to see you looking so much better again.' She took his hand in hers.

He gave a little laugh. 'It'd take more than one bullet to put me down.' He paused, moving his mending body into a more comfortable position. He stared at Gina for a moment, frowning slightly at the dark shadows under her eyes and acknowledging silently what she must have been through. The knowledge brought anger with it, and for a moment he closed his lids again, dwelling on the memory of Demetrios and the way he had seen him last – a red, bloody mess at his feet. But he could remember nothing else! His mind was blank. 'What happened back there? It's a bit blurry to me yet. Who shot me?'

'Santana.'

'Did they get him?'

'Yes. And the Dutchmen. It's all over, Perez. We won.'

'Is your dad okay?'

'He's fine. He's outside now, and he wants to see you.'

'And Baxter? What about Baxter?'

She threw him a quick glance. 'What about him?'

'Is he ... Is he right out of the picture?'

'He was never in it.'

'But, in the beginning, I thought ...'

'Well, you thought wrong. Mark asked me to marry him once, but it would never have worked. Not in a million years.'

'Why?'

'He's not my type.'

'Who is your type, Gina?'

'I think you know the answer to that.' She smiled briefly, gathering up her bag and opening it to bring out some papers. 'Look, I've a present for you.'

'What is it?'

'Can't you guess?'

Perez squinted at the papers, reaching out to take them and opening them up. His tired eyes scanned the contents, then he turned back to Gina. 'I can't believe it. Where did you find them?'

She grinned. 'You know, Perez, it always amazes me how much trouble a girl can get into, just minding her own business. There I was, plain old Gina Matheson ...'

'Plain?'

'Well, fairly plain. Anyway, there I was, simply wanting to do something for the forests and meeting this fabulous guy who was to take me there, and the next thing I'm in the middle of a drugs ring, gun-running, hostile Indians etc etc ...'

'Stop it! Where did you find the papers?'

'You'll never believe it!'

'Try me!' Perez squeezed her hand. 'You should know by now I'll believe anything you tell me.' It was an instant bond. 'Where did you find them?'

Gina looked down at him and loved him, every crazy little

thing about him. And he loved her. That was the most marvellous thing of all. And no matter what happened from now on, nothing would ever be the same again for either of them. She gave a little shrug. 'They were in my camera case.'

He stared at her, incredulous. 'In your *camera case*?'

'Yes.' She swallowed, glancing at his face before she went on. 'When I came home from the hospital, after leaving you here ...' she swallowed again '... the police had left my things with my father. They told me later that, while we were on the plane, they cleared up the mess at the air strip. They pulled the Toyota and the truck to pieces, and they found my backpacks in the boot of the truck and sent them on – minus something very important they'd discovered. My camera case. We – Dad and I – were called in, of course. To be interviewed.' She hesitated. She had been wondering how to tell him about Elena.

'Tell me all of it, Gina!'

'I'll try, but I don't know the exact details, except that Elena was found by some Indians. She was half dead. Evidently Sinon had abandoned her in the forest. Elena finally confessed that she'd been trying to frame me by stuffing the papers into my camera case. She was hoping that they'd find them on me and think I was part of the plot. But that didn't happen. My dad got me out of it by ...'

'You don't have to explain to me how the company works.' She winced. 'This time I approve.'

'She's very ill now. Critical. Here in the hospital. I don't think she's going to get over it, Perez. But she did confess.' Her candid eyes stared into his. 'Are you very upset? You cared for her once.'

He lifted his eyebrows at her. 'Yes. Once. Until I found out what she was like. I'm no more sorry for her than I'd be sorry for any woman holed up in some forest hut. Or any human would be about another's ordeal. You need have no fears of that. Remember, I knew what Elena was like. And even though she confessed, I'm sure it wasn't for you, darling. Although it seems harsh, I'm pretty sure it was because she thought she was on her way out. I expect she still hoped I might forgive her.'

They fell silent for a moment, sitting quietly holding hands. Perez let Gina's words sink in. Who would have thought of looking in Gina's camera case? Certainly, not Sinon! Nor Santana!

'And I shan't be going to see her! Do you feel better now?' he added.

'Perez!'

'I want you to know that I love you with the whole of my heart.'

'I do. And, for what it's worth, I'm sorry for Elena too.' They kissed. 'At least with those papers on offer, we've been able to put Santana away for a long time. I only wish Sinon could have paid for his crimes in court.'

'It was the best thing, how it ended. God knows I hated the man, but I wouldn't have envied him rotting away for years in some disgusting gaol,' he replied.

She added, 'These papers are only copies, of course. The originals are with the police. They're too damning to risk another loss. But I wanted you to see them.'

'I'm glad I have.'

A soft tap came on the door, and they both looked up. Perez grinned a little ruefully. 'More visitors, by the sound of it.'

'It's probably Dad. Shall I tell him to go away? Surely you're tired now?'

'A bit, but I'd like to see him.'

'Or it could be the doctor coming to drive me away from you.'

'Wild horses couldn't do that,' he grinned. 'Better see who it is.

'Come in!'

The door opened and Colin Matheson's head appeared. 'Feeling better, Perez?'

'Much better, Matheson. Nice to see you.'

'When you're up to it, we'd like to have a word.'

'*We*?'

'The company.'

Perez frowned slightly. 'I can't imagine what the company and I have to say to each other.'

'I think you might be surprised. Anyway, there's time enough for that. In the meantime, there's someone here who is desperate to say hello.'

'Who's that, then?'

Colin opened the door a little wider and, standing there, a broad grin on his little, dark face, was Luis.

'Hello, lady! Hello, Perez! I've brought you one of my stitches for a present.'

'*Luis!*' Gina leapt up with a delighted cry and rushed to embrace the little Indian boy. His leg was bound and splinted, and the crutches under his arms were a little on the big side for such a small boy. He hobbled forward, his hand proudly holding out the spiky suture, and gave it to Perez. He was used to seeing Gina. She had called in to see him on her daily visits to Perez. And she knew that he'd had skin grafts to his leg and that, before too long, he would be back home.

'Well, thank you, Luis,' Perez was saying, grinning as he gingerly took the stitch. 'That was very thoughtful of you.'

'Are my stitches as big as yours?' Perez laughed.

'I don't know. I'll have to compare them when they take mine out.'

Four weeks later, sitting at the bar in one of Belem's more intimate nightspots, Gina twirled the stem of her wineglass and looked across at Perez. 'Are you going to take the job, then?'

Perez regarded Gina. He knew what she was asking him, but he didn't know how to answer. She looked beautiful that night. Her shining hair was catching the light like a halo, her blue eyes sparkled and her whole beautiful being seemed alight with happiness. This girl by his side that night was a far cry from the Gina he'd known in the Xingu. He was remembering the stained, faded shirt and the jeans tucked into the mud-spattered boots.

After what she'd been through, would she ever be able to face going back there? If not, then he would have to resign himself to a life in the city with her. It was not a decision he'd arrived at easily. But Gina was more important to him now than anything else – even the forest – and he would have no choice.

She took his hand, squeezing it for a moment before taking a sip of her wine, then looked at him and searched his unsmiling face. 'Darling, please don't look at me like that. There's so much to look forward to now.'

He sat there for a moment, absolutely still. 'It was good to hear about the company deciding to change its ways.'

'Yes, my dad had a lot to do with that, persuading them to stick to rubber again.'

He grinned. 'I know. And I think the tax incentives had something to do with it, as well. Still, what does it matter, if they're on our side at last? At least I got some great compensation, as well as their promise.'

'Whatever their reason, they're committed now to saving the forests, and that can't be a bad thing, can it?'

'Of course not. And it was good of them to offer me the job, but …' He stopped then, not knowing how to ask her.

'But?' She smiled patiently, then reached out again to take his other hand, finding the words for him. 'The way I see it,' she said softly, 'is that if we have to go all the way back to take Luis home, we might as well look the job over.' She leaned back on the steel rails of the bar seat. 'Besides, I think I'd rather like to be the wife of a ranger. And how many kids would have a back-yard like ours?'

'It would mean a lot of hard work. It wouldn't be easy keeping an eye on the poachers and the squatters. It would mean years and years of living on the edge of the forest.'

'I can't think of anywhere I'd rather be.'

'What about your books? And your photography?'

She shrugged. 'What about them? There's nothing to stop me writing in the forest, is there?'

'No. But …'

'Perez, don't ask me to marry you and expect me to stay in the city. It'd kill me. I'm not being noble, truly. I love the interior every bit as much as you do.'

'Do you? Won't you find it lonely?'

'No, I won't. I've made a lot of friends, remember. In fact, it may get a little too crowded at times, what with Fred and Sheila, Caninde and Jeronimo, not to mention the other Indians I've got to know. Now, stop looking so worried!' she added. 'Finish your drink and take me back to my flat. We're getting married tomorrow, so we need an early night. Besides, it's been six hours since we made love, Perez.'

'I think this is the time you can call me Rafe!' he grinned.

'Rafe,' she said, lingering over the word. 'I wonder why I didn't ask your first name before? I suppose "Perez" suited you, because you were always so grumpy.' Fun glinted in her eyes, then they became serious. 'I love you.' They smiled at each other, savouring the joke.

Perez felt peace then. Real peace. It was the same peace he had felt the very first time he'd ever entered the forest. He took her hand and brought it gently to his lips. Tomorrow they were going to be married, and then they'd be going back together to the Xingu.

He was taking Gina home!

About the Author

Helen McCabe is a highly regarded author whose love of writing and powerful imagination, coupled with a determination to succeed, have ensured a long and successful career. Her lifelong fascination with literature, history and research and an interest in the paranormal have enhanced Helen's immense gift for creative storytelling.

She graduated with Honours from London University, where she read English, and holds an MA degree in 18th Century English Literature from the University of Keele.

Her long career began with her first novel at the age of seven, with poetry published at 13 and read on BBC radio. She started her true career as a novelist after becoming well-known for her short stories and serials in popular magazines. In 1995 her first full-length novel – *Two for a Lie*, about the 19th Century Princess Caraboo – was published, gaining much interest and critical acclaim. Since then, in tandem with work and family, she has written more than 30 novels in various genres, including historical, romance and more recently horror/thriller and crime. She also writes scripts for film, television and the stage.

Alongside her writing, Helen has worked in a variety of jobs, beginning as an assistant librarian and finally as a lecturer and teacher. She is a member of the Romantic Novelists Association, the Crime Writers' Association, the Horror Writers of America and the West Country Writers' Association.

Helen was invited to join Mensa, the high IQ Society, in 1989.

Helen lives in Worcester and has three grown-up children and a grandson.

Her website is at www.helenmccabe.com.

Other Titles from Telos Moonrise

ROMANTIC ENCOUNTERS

Helen McCabe
The Price of Love
In Search of Love
Hostage to Love
When Love Rides Out
Highway of Fear
A Garden Fair
The House on the Mountain

Juliette Benzoni
Catherine: One Love is Enough
Catherine
Belle Catherine
Catherine and Arnaud
Catherine and a Time for Love
A Snare for Catherine
The Lady of Montsalvy

SINFUL PLEASURES

Awakening Jessica by Athena Michaels
Byte Me! by Roberta Steele
Witchcraven by Kate Dennis